BURIED ROSES BLOOM
(A COLD CASE)

Theresa Quarles

Buried Roses Bloom

Copyright © 2022 Theresa Quarles

All rights reserved. No part of this publication may be reproduced or transmitted in any form or by any means without the written permission of the publisher. All rights reserved.

ISBN: 978-1-956884-04-3

Contributing Editor: or all services completed by Imprint Productions, Inc.

Cover Design: or all services completed by Imprint Productions, Inc.

Printed in the United States of America

Published by Imprint Productions, Inc.

First Edition 2022

DEDICATION

*This book is dedicated in the
The memory of my mother,
Annie Bell Haynes Quarles
I feel she is smiling down on me from
the Heavens.*

*My Grandmother, Alma Blunt Haynes
My Grandfather, Ralph Haynes
My Cousin, Archie Alphonso Alexander*

ACKNOWLEDGMENT

Buried Rose Blooms is a fictional novel based on a true story. This book has dramatized characters who tried to live ordinary lives. It is intended for the reader to grasp the events being shared as if they were a part of the very thing that was happening. My hope is to leave the reader with the feeling of meeting destiny through the expression of the written word.

I would like to thank the following people starting with my cousin and editor, Stephanie Cavett and Jennifer Howard-Tate. These ladies both have sharp eyes, unique creativity, passion, and love for editing by direction of their quiet wisdom.

A special thank you to my daughter, Crystal Quarles McDowell for the poem that she wrote expressing much energy and beauty that flowed straight from her heart.

Lastly, I'm grateful to Mr. Martin and my uncle Henry Brown. I give credit to these two men who managed to steer me in the gentlest way, leading me in the right direction. Their willingness to share their information with me will always be appreciated.

A SILENT CRY FROM HEAVEN

A rampage of racial clusters surrounded us.
There was nowhere left to run and no reason to put up more of a fuss.

The lives we led before this day are now complete.
We thought we had promising futures, but we couldn't outrun this defeat.

The jealousy of those who felt we had too much,
robbed us of everything and left our families with not even a future to trust.
Even though we had no material items they wanted,
they always found reasons to kill us. So, we felt haunted.

Like a circus, they paraded us around town for all to see,
and hung our bodies lifelessly from a tree.

It was known that no Black man should be better off than any white man alive.
But we had to stand up for ourselves. We had to try.

Someone had to attempt to live a better life,
to overcome the ignorance and strife.
For our bodies were left uncovered.
Leaving us no dignity to muster.

Our families were never given the chance to say goodbye,
and no gravesite is present to visit or to sit beside.

Although no solid evidence of our stories
are apparent. Always know that we were there
and let their manipulative ways be transparent.

Continue to fight the lifelong struggle of racism,
because as long as there is a devil in hell, there
will always be someone there to challenge the truths we tell.

By: Crystal Quarles McDowell

Chapter 1
Real Good Times

At the beginning of 1927 there were sawmills all over Lincoln County, Mississippi - specifically the town of Brookhaven. A sawmill is where timber is sawn into planks and boards. By using this type of process, it makes it marketable. If you were to work in one of these sawmills, you would be paid one dollar a day.

The Timber Checkers would be paid from one dollar and fifty cents to two dollars a day. There was plenty of work because of these sawmills. Lumber was a valuable business for all involved. The workers had to wear particular items every day for their safety. Those items included: highlighted suspenders, steel toe boots, safety glasses, hard hats and gloves all day while working. This is a routine dressing code from season to season. During this time, legislatures were farmers; they passed the laws to suit themselves. Lawmakers refused to allow any millworker to get wealthy from their sawmill pay. If that had happened, they could intervene, as far as the labor was concerned. This is how the legislatures kept their farmland laborers in bondage and it made it hard for them to leave. As a result, the legislatures kept control of the workers and maintained a bare minimum pay.

Hotels had a great business and so did the meat markets. There was one meat market, south of Brookhaven, called the South Side Meat Market, owned by a young man named Terry Lee Hardy. Terry was a fast talker who always had a story people wanted to hear. Terry once had a customer who had made a purchase, but he was still there listening and wanting more to the very end. In other words, Terry's stories were mouth-watering.

There was a ringing at the door as more customers entered. That's when Terry Hardy does his best performance. Terry would weigh the meat of his customer and unknowingly, you will be paying for the weight of his hand pressing down on the meat scale. While he blinded them with his shucking and jiving, they're laughing and having fun, not knowing they were the victims of circumstance. Customers would end up paying for two pounds of meat and one pound of Terry's hand that would be weighing down the meat. Business was good for Terry.

All over Mississippi, there were trees with vines running around and through them. Colorful wildflowers scattered all over with wild berries and plenty of critters to explore. But Terry Lee Hardy, who loved nature, didn't have the time for some of the things he loved because his lifestyle didn't allow it.
Despite his immoral business practices, Terry was a man who loved his family and would do everything to keep their life in

a pleasant state. Terry enjoyed working in his meat market. He could not imagine the idea of spending half of a day or even every day working, doing something that he hated. He knew that would have consequences dragging behind it. For it would defeat the purpose of living a long and healthy life and he loved living.

When customers walked into the meat market for the first time, they would immediately notice the fresh smell of the store. The next thing they noticed was Terry's red, fiery hair. Terry's hair swept each side of his temple as he moved swiftly to complete the orders as they were made. Terry certainly had his faults, but he was an excellent businessman who knew how to work his magic, especially in a crowd. As the customers steadily entered into the meat market, Terry had that look of confidence about him as he moved. He managed to service his customers to their satisfaction as quickly as they entered. Everything ran smoothly because of his employee loyalty and willingness to help. Terry knew that he was doing something right.

Terry married Marilyn Hardy one beautiful Sunday afternoon on June 22, 1919. Terry recalled feeling that all over the world, lucky couples were getting married too. His face never ceased to light up when his eyes met hers. Terry thought of that beautiful day often. How beautiful she was with her golden wavy hair that was pulled up under her veil, with just small portions that hung down her shoulders and down the side of each of her curvy rose-tone cheeks.

Her wedding dress was a beige color in satin material with lace that swept the floor beautifully behind her. The smell of that woman alone was intoxicating. He could hardly wait until the wedding was over so that he could be alone with the woman who always made him feel nothing but loved.

Just as Terry thought things couldn't get any better, a year later, they had a son and they named him Matthew Hardy. Matthew had a head of luxurious red hair that you just could not ignore. In other words, his hair was like his father's. At the age of seven, Matthew was the mirror image of his father, right down to his big blue eyes and his narrow face.

Terry did what he thought would make them happy and that was spending as much time together as being active and full of life, with his family. Matthew enjoyed their family gatherings, this very thing always put a smile on that little innocent face. Terry was known for his ability to multitask; he would be setting in motion a plan to elude the current routine to something enticing as well as its being exciting.

It was on a Tuesday afternoon when Terry came up with a great idea for the family while he was hard at work. He was going to surprise them with it. As it was about that time for the meat market to close, the bell on the door rang. Terry looked up and all he could see was that bright, blazing light from the sun, shining through. Then there was a break, and he could see someone and that someone was Mark Child, a dear friend of his.

Terry said while laughing, "What a surprise man," as he came out from behind the counter and shook Marks' hand. They wouldn't stay away from one another long before one would visit the other. That's how close they were and have always had great times hanging out together. Even when they were kids, they hardly ever got into trouble, but that was because they hardly ever got caught.

Mark followed Terry into his office and took a seat. Terry took two glasses out from the bar, placed them on top of the counter, pouring the Scotch Whiskey swiftly and it looked like the flow of a waterfall. Terry handed Mark his glass of whiskey and Mark stood up to make a toast. When their glasses clicked, they shouted, "For the sake of love and money."

The men took a seat, Mark asked Terry if he read the newspaper recently. He was referring to "The Lincoln County Times." Terry didn't want to sound like he didn't read the newspaper at all. So, his answer was not recent, and from that, he asked what's going on.

After reading an article in the newspaper, Mark felt like it was his duty to give Terry a visit. He mentioned there was an article that announced the Ku Klux Klan will be speaking Tuesday, February 22, 1927. "Take a guess where the meeting is?"

Terry didn't have a clue. He replied, "Umm….out in the country maybe."

Mark didn't hesitate to respond with, "Heck no, the meeting is right here in Brookhaven, that's the convenient side about it."

Terry couldn't believe what he was hearing. He thought Mark was bullshitting him, so he asked him. Mark told Terry that he knows how he feels but the news was in black and white. This meeting would be held behind the Post Office but in case it rains it would be held at Brookhaven High School Auditorium, at 6:00 p.m. Terry looked at Mark, then he took a sip of his whiskey, and his next words were, "Aw shit."
Mark was just honest; he admits he's curious. Mark thinks they should go, so he promises to pick Terry up. "This would be our first time witnessing something like that my friend," Mark stated.

Terry replied, "Yep, I can hardly wait, literally."

Mark laughed as he lifted his glass up to his lips and drank the last drop of whiskey. Mark stood up and Terry did the same, they started walking towards the door. Terry expressed how great the idea was to come up with something interesting to attend, as he opened the door. Mark shook Terry's hand and said, "Man it's like that every time we meet," as he headed to his car.

Terry locked up the meat market and was out the door at nearly the same time as Mark. Like clockwork, he always went home, for he was a happy man.

From the moment Terry opened the South Side Meat Market, Thursday morning Feb.17, 1927, at 8:00 a.m. the bell on the door never stopped ringing. He didn't know what to think. He thought, "Maybe a large number of people decided to take off from work today and made this day to do their shopping and stop by my place."

There were as many familiar faces as those unfamiliar, entering and exiting the meat market. This was the perfect time for Terry to perform his money-making strategy and he worked it like a charm. After all, Terry had years of putting it in motion. He always stood near the scale with his apron on, as he weighed the meat and rang it up, while his employee did the rest.

The business was at its peak. It had become overwhelming for Terry and that made him proud. Terry had been so busy that he didn't have time to think about a story and if he did, he wouldn't have had enough time for the story part of the plan to be put in motion. But now, he thought, now is the time to put it in motion. Since Terry could see through the crowd and the rush was in demand, he started talking a mile a minute to one of his customers. Terry and this customer touched on a subject about racing cars and that's how it started, and this is how it ended.

Terry began saying that there was a young man who drove a huge car, called a Six Studebaker and it was an excellent car. "I can say, it reminded me of a woman because it turned many heads and put a smile on their faces. "After that, laughter filled the room. He continued, "As you know, it is hard passing through town without getting stopped by the law. Sometimes you're glad to see them and sometimes you're not."

Someone made a comment and said, "He's right about that," and heads were nodding.

Terry continued, "All of a sudden, right in the middle of town, the driver of the Six Studebaker failed to stop; and he went straight through the stop sign. A police car appeared behind it almost immediately with the sirens on. The officers attempted to force the driver to stop but the driver never showed any sign of stopping any time soon. In fact, that's when he pressed the accelerator, and man those tires were spinning, squealing, and smoking like they were on fire. That's when the driver earned the name Road Runner. The officers thought the name Road Runner best described the character driving the car. The Road Runner drove wild and crazy, and was a very bold and ambitious one. Being stopped by officers wasn't on the Road Runner's mind, certainly not that day. Oh boy! Didn't the Road Runner give those officers a good ole time? The officers chased the Road Runner a total of nineteen miles, and it ended near Nola Road."

"Hell, they wanted him bad." Someone hollered out.

Terry continued, "The Road Runner was revealed as Samson DeLaughter. He lived out west of Brookhaven. Samson had his wife and two children traveling alone with him too."

A voice out of the crowd shouted, "What a fool of a man to drive like that with his family with him."

Terry continued, "The officers searched the car, and a shipment of booze was confiscated. The monster of a car contained three hundred quarts of White Horse Cellar whiskey.

Marshall Owens and police officer Lee were with Sheriff Brice when they made the arrest. The officers had gotten a tip that led to DeLaughter's arrest. He was put in jail and the whiskey went in the Sheriff's vault."

There was an immediate response from one of the customers. He was puzzled over what happens to the whiskey after it leaves the vault. He wanted to invest in a business of getting rid of evidence management, and everyone laughed. Terry thought, maybe that's a promising idea as he thanked one of his customers for his purchase.

The customer in return just wanted to thank him for not charging for the story too. Terry smiled thinking, but I did charge you. Then he thanked him and told him how he appreciated him and to come back again. Then Terry thought, if he only knew.

Before Terry stopped for the day, three guys entered the meat market. Terry recognized one of them as Guy Martin and the other two men looked to be his age, in their thirties. They wanted to make a purchase and they did. They were friendly and very talkative, which made them stand out. Guy Martin with a smile on his face introduced his friends to Terry as two fine brothers, Michael and Herbert Tucker.

Both of the men were tall with skin like brown sugar. Michael had mentioned that they were back home from being in the Military. Terry enjoyed talking to them, and it was mostly about their life in the military. Terry thought the conversation was fascinating. Now Terry found himself listening to one of the finest stories that deserved attention. Terry thanked the brothers for sharing a piece of their experience with him. "Now that's what I would call really supporting our country," Terry said.

Michael expressed the idea of actually being on duty with so much death around him most of the time. He also stressed the word death because that was no joking matter. He knew it would have to be something you wanted to do or go into it thinking that it's something that you can do. He stated, "You will be faced with death and surrounded by this crucial reality that's suddenly before you. In order to handle all of that chaos you really would be better off if you painted at least a mental picture at first in your mind. It needs to be the worst and the craziest thing that comes to your mind, that's what helped me." Michael continued, "By the way, staying alive is at the top of that reality stage. Not everyone is military material, so you will have disturbing moments that we caused on ourselves. That might sound erratic but in a twisted way, it's just like that."

After listening to Michael, Terry could see that picture he painted and how much sense it made. His perception was clear. Terry explained that after going through something of that magnitude; when you wake up every morning someone should be standing at the foot of your bed. He should be ready to salute you and I mean, every morning. He felt like you should have earned that right, at least. It takes a man with a huge heart to carry some psycho shit on their shoulder. Terry stood straight and gave a salute to the brothers.

The brothers were touched like you wouldn't believe. Michael appreciated hearing the truth when real feelings are being shared. Hearing words being expressed in that way is powerful. A part of you heals every time you hear powerful words. When we speak, we should be careful what we say because we never know what state that person's mind is in. They were overwhelmed with gratitude for such wonderful words. They really enjoyed the conversation like they would enjoy their purchases. They thanked Terry as they were about

to exit. Terry asked Guy to bring them back. Terry stated, "They're always welcome here." Guy didn't have a problem with that because he knew they had to eat. They all laughed as they headed out of the door.

That bell on the door rang for the last customer of the day. The workers were clearing the building as was Terry. Terry didn't have words to describe, what a day it had been. But he managed to realize it had been a long one. As he and his headman, Lawrence Smith, were shaking their heads as they were exiting the building. Lawrence's words were that everyone was satisfied, as usual, and to have a good evening and will meet again the next day. The crew knew they were doing great in business because of the tremendous orders. They knew they were putting out great work and the business was looking up. Terry thanked everyone for being so loyal on another "prosperous day."

When things are going extremely well the body reacts right along with those feelings. Terry knows that yesterday's result was impressive. Now, today it's looking like the same change reaction. Terry knows it pays to go with the flow and that's what he did. This Friday, February 18, 1927, he worked all day with the emotion and the excitement of how the heavenly gates had opened up to him.

It was 5:30 p.m. when the last customer left the meat market. Terry was dragging his feet until he made it to his car. He got into his car and started driving. The next thing you know, Terry started singing "This was a great d-a-y today. I can still hear the drawer of the cash register ringing, ding, ding, ding, and a ding, all day long, ding." Terry kept singing until he reached his destination, home. Terry noticed it was too quiet for anyone to be there as he entered.

That's when he heard a noise that seemed to be coming from Matthew's bedroom. Terry went for his forty-five, caliber pistol that was in the China cabinet in the dining room. He took the safety off of the gun first then he called the police to be on the safe side, as he hung up the phone. Terry started walking slowly in the direction of Matthew's bedroom. His eyes were moving quickly to every angle of the room, and he didn't see anything or anyone. He quickly moved to the bed as he stooped down and looked under it, there was no one there. He got up and moved to the closet, grabbed the doorknob, and pulled the door open. A baseball bat was leaning against the door, so when Terry opened the door, the bat fell to the floor. That's when Terry's heart started pumping really fast. Then he picked up the bat and placed it back in the closet.

After Terry closed the door, all of a sudden Terry felt pressure on his body. Terry found himself going down fast to the floor with no control and the forty-five went in one direction and he went in another. Terry was receiving blows to his head from the left then to right. The burglar got off of Terry and Terry struggled over to his gun that was lying by the closet door. On his knees, he pointed the forty-five at the burglar. The burglar was about to escape through the window as Terry yelled, as he stood up on his feet saying, "Before you touch that ground, you will be filled with bullets you son-of-a-bitch." Terry had the burglar get on his knees as he couldn't resist punching the burglar, giving him just what he needed.

Terry wanted him to never forget this moment, breaking into his home. He was punching him as he spoke. The police finally arose, Terry yelled, "I'm in the bedroom." That's when Terry lowered his hand letting down his defense. The police officer handcuffed the burglar while the other one read him his rights, then they made a report on what had happened.

Terry left the window open and told the officers that's how the burglar entered their home. There were other officers looking around the premises inside and out. "Wild!" Terry said as he grabbed his head with his left hand while still holding the gun in the other hand. He had to come in through my son's bedroom window.

One of the police officers told Terry he had done a great

job. "The best thing about it all, is your family was not here and they are safe. It could have been a different story here today. You have a damn good weapon for protection Mr. Hardy. We will place the report on file, and we will be patrolling the area still just in case. If you need us again, don't hesitate to call us as you did." They shook Terry's hand and drove off. Terry was able to take a long, overdue bath and take a nap.

Chapter 2
A Wonderful Surprise

A few hours had passed, by the time the rest of the family made it home. Matthew was running to the door waiting for his mother to open it. As soon as she opened the door, Matthew ran through the house looking for his father. He found him finally lying in his bed. As soon as Matthew reached the side of the bed where his father was lying, Matthew just stared at him. His daddy opened one eye and made a roaring sound as he jumped out of the bed and grabbed Matthew up in his arms. Laugher was all over the room as they landed back in the bed. Marilyn was standing in the doorway admiring the two most important people in her life. Matthew and Terry looked over at Marilyn standing there laughing. Terry sat up in the bed with Matthew and told Marilyn that he had to show them a thing or two. To their surprise, Terry took them off in the car. Marilyn couldn't take it anymore after they started heading north. Terry never mentioned what had transpired earlier.

Marilyn really wanted to know where they were going, but

she was trying to be clever about it. Matthew didn't care, he just shouted from the back seat, "Dad where are we going?"

Terry keeps driving telling them that both of them are being kidnapped and he's taken them to his chamber. Matthew being the boy he was, wanted to know what kidnapping meant? So, Terry being the kidnapper took it upon himself to explain what it meant.

You know Matthew, "Kidnapping is only fun when your mother or me is doing it. Otherwise, no one else can get away with kidnapping you. I will take you places, and you won't know where I'm taking you until we get there. My son, kidnapping would be like I'm doing with you right now, we would just be having fun. Like your mother, she wouldn't want anyone else but me to kidnap her. Matthew, your mother loved being kidnapped by me."

Matthew thought his dad was funny but understood everything he said. Marilyn kissed Terry on his cheek and laid her head on his shoulder. When they reached their destination, they were in front of a motel called The Stars. Terry went inside and came out with a key that had the number twenty on it. He was so excited; nothing could ruin that moment for Terry because it meant everything to him. He drove around to the other side of the motel. Terry opened the car door, leaned over and kissed Marilyn on her lips, and whispered her name, and she awoke. He reached for Matthew and placed him on his shoulder and carried him because he was asleep. Terry reached for Marilyn's hand, and they entered their suite. Terry had everything they needed as he went to get their clothes out of the car. Everyone got ready for bed, asked no question, and went right to sleep, like in the story of "The Three Bears".

Now the next day was a whole other story. When Marilyn was woken up that Saturday morning by her husband, she was at her favorite motel with breakfast being served. These were significant times for the family to relax with each other and show appreciation for one another, as a family. Terry's theory went like this: if you show love and if love is there for you, it's possible that you'll receive great love. That's what Terry was about, taking that extra step.

After breakfast, Matthew was the first to get dressed. His face was all smiles as he modeled for his parents to show how good he dressed. They applauded their little red-headed angel. In a matter of minutes, everyone was ready to exit. They happily got into the car. Marilyn and Matthew were ready for just about anything, as long as it was stimulating. Marilyn thanked her husband for being so philosophical. Now, that didn't stop her from wanting to know where they were going. Terry laughed knowing that the both of them were ridiculous. Terry knows that he has this in the bag, but Marilyn wanted him to know that she's trying to pull it out of the bag, "honey."

"Yell! Out of the bag Dad," said Matthew. The two didn't know what to anticipate, they didn't have a clue.

After driving for hours, they were in Kentucky and

Terry parked at this huge museum. People were coming from every direction to that particular spot. Terry paid for tickets at the booth, and they walked right into the building. Before long, Terry found their seats. Now Matthew and his mother were doing a lot of whispering. Terry was just sitting there with this smile on his face. He knew by the expression of joy on their faces, his attempt was achieved.

There were young men who were carrying trays that were supported by a strap that went around their neck. As one of the men came closer, Terry raised his hand and one of the young men responded. Each one of them chose the object that they wanted to light up in the dark. Terry wanted a souvenir to remind them of this moment. Matthew helped himself to a bag of popcorn while the grownups preferred peanuts. People were steadily coming as if something amazing was about to occur.

There were lots of moving going on before the seats were all filled. The lights were dim and there was silence but only for a slight moment. Then there was this rumbling sound that felt like someone was sitting in your chest with a set of drums, banging on it. It certainly was a circus. All of a sudden there were big lights flashing all around. You could see people only when the lights flashed on them where they were seated. Then the flashing of the lights stopped, there were tigers in their cages.

Matthew was so excited to see the huge, beautiful tigers in the center of the floor surrounded by a huge cage. There was a man to each tiger performing tricks and there were three of them. But the one that placed his head in the tiger's mouth had everyone up in their seats. Matthew was most excited watching the clowns on stilts. He was enchanted, watching the way they moved. Matthew was right there with him as if he were in a trance. He didn't know what to think, all he could say was "Wow! Look, mom."

Marilyn was more than pleased with the circus and Terry feeling mutual as he knew he was the man in charge. The show lasted for three hours and there wasn't a dull moment. Marilyn and Terry were just as astonished as Matthew was or more. Matthew talked about the circus all the way to the car. Terry drove off with caution out of the parking lot. All you could see were the back patron's cars, and they were heading in all directions.

Marilyn wanted to know what the next plan was, and she asked but she knew she wouldn't get an answer. Terry never answered the question. He just kept driving as if he never heard her. After driving a ways, Terry came to a red light and stopped. Marilyn looked around and she recognized the area. She hesitated only for a moment then she knew where her husband was taking them now, and on her birthday, February 19, 1927. She looked at him with those big eyes. "Oh, honey, we are in Ohio. You are taking us to Aunt Helen's house right, Honey, I love you so much," as their lips touch with a kiss.

Then Matthew expressed his feeling by telling his dad

that he loved him too. Then Terry told his son that he loved him more. He drove on with confidence and a smile on his face. There was joy all around them as they approached Aunt Helen's home.

Aunt Helen was overjoyed when she opened the door. They hadn't seen one another in over a year. Aunt Helen would hug them, then she would look at them, then she would hug them again. She couldn't believe how fast Matthew had grown because she knew she wasn't getting any older. Aunt Helen started out with her favorite words, time waits for no one, which meant that she had a lot to catch up on, in a short length of time. Terry knew they could talk forever but he didn't have that much patience for that right then. All he wanted to hear was let's go to a restaurant. So being the man that he was, he decided to bring the subject to the light.

Terry started talking on the subject of Aunt Helen's favorite restaurant, how magnificently each bite will taste. It took about a minute and that idea was flying high. Oh boy, those were the keywords, and he didn't have to say it twice. Terry knew right then and there that they were going to be eating an exquisite meal at his Aunt Helen's favorite restaurant and soon. There was a huge smile on his face.

Matthew was elated by just the thought of being in the same presence with his aunt again. Helen got a sweater out of the closet and put it on. She took Matthew by his hand, and they all headed out the door. Terry stopped at the service station to service the car and they were off again. Helen expressed herself very well and quite frequently. She talked about everything. The significance of it all, everyone knew how much they were loved and missed by her.

Marilyn thought the world of her aunt. She was her idol as she turned around to look at her; she was as beautiful as ever. Her light brown hair hung on her shoulder with waves that were so deep, so perfect with the most beautiful glow, especially when the sun shined on it. Her hair even matched her hazel eyes. Marilyn knows her son can see the good in her. Children can see those things in people, plus, she treats him with much love.

Aunt Helen was the one that made it the special place because when they would go out to eat, she would suggest the place to go. After they were being served such wonderful meals there, to keep going back was the only right thing to do. So, they all called it Aunt Helen's favorite restaurant.

They finally reached Miller's Restaurant and they all were sitting around a table that shared a huge window with a distant view of people doing their daily chores. Everyone ordered their favorite steaks and the way they wanted it, but Matthew preferred his old fashion hamburger. He would say how it just melts in his mouth. And his face would just light up.

Matthew told Aunt Helen about the circus and how his father surprised his mom and himself. He let her know how much fun he had and all of the entertainment there to see. Matthew told her how he didn't want to leave, and "Mom didn't want to leave either." Aunt Helen reached over and pinched Matthew on his cheek and smiled then he blushed.

Marilyn agreed it was exceptionally good and she enjoyed it, the lions were her favorite and Matthew was infatuated with the lions and the clowns. He actually wanted to take them home. He just couldn't get enough. He didn't want that moment to end.

After Aunt Helen heard everyone's moments of excitement, she was impressed the most, from what she heard about Terry. While listening to her loved one, all she could hear was how Terry handled everything with so much grace. She loves the fact that he was very generous, but most of all, he's considerate toward his family, which within itself means a lot. That unconditional love is awesome. Aunt Helen let Marilyn know that "He's a hell of a man. That baby is100%. He just needs to keep that up, it will pay off in the long run. Damn, that's paying off now."

Marilyn thanked her aunt for those special remarks that she couldn't express any better herself and thanked her for speaking the truth about her husband, saying the nicest things. Terry didn't know what they were talking about. Terry made an announcement that their food was about to be served. Marilyn thought he was so funny, acting like he didn't notice what was being said. She knew he had to be tickled over everything that was shared and it was all about him too. He was looking rather unconcerned, but he handled it rather nonchalantly.

The waitress had a tray of food and the smell of it could fill you up. It was quiet for a brief moment before Aunt Helen was back to talking again. She wanted Terry to understand the importance of what he's doing and how he treats his family is very special. She stated, "When a person is doing good by their family or he tries to do everything he can for his family, they need to hear that. There is nothing more important or looks so sophisticated than a handsome man, who cares for his beautiful family. Not just looking the part but actually taking care of his family. When you are in love with someone and taking care of that person is what you do naturally but some of us may need a push every now and then. In doing that, you could save a marriage or save a life. We just never know. When you care about someone and you know that they're doing wrong, then you feel like you have an obligation to let them know or at least talk about it."

Matthew was listening, he told them when he does wrong, that his mom and dad tells him when he's doing wrong and he says, he listens to. They all laughed, and the atmosphere was delightful. The timing was perfect, the food was exquisite, and the conversation was, well let just say that Aunt Helen felt it was all so good.

Terry looked at the time and said to himself, "Where did the time go?. Right now, Terry felt like he had written a prescription for time, and it played out exactly the way he wanted. After Terry had taken care of the bill, they were on their way back to Aunt Helen's home. Marilyn noticed that her aunt seemed somewhat different, she couldn't explain it. She thought, maybe we should visit more often.

When Terry drove up to the house, everyone got out of the car and Marilyn got closer to Terry and gave him a quick kiss on his cheek and she suggested if they could spend some extra time with their Aunt Helen. "What do you think about that, honey?"

Terry wanted the both of them to just get inside and relax for a minute. Terry opened the door for his family and there was this loud shouting saying, "Happy Birthday!" Then they heard, "Happy Birthday to you. Happy Birthday to you! Happy Birthday dear Marilyn! Happy Birthday to you!"

Marilyn's mouth was wide open with surprise. She kept saying, "No way, no way, you really got me. I didn't have a clue."

Everyone kept singing Happy Birthday to Marilyn. Marilyn couldn't believe it, but she was very exhilarated. She was speechless as Terry picked Matthew up in his arms. Then he grabbed Marilyn by her hand and led the way to the birthday cake. Terry looked at the cake then he looked at the wife and she was speechless. Terry wants her to really look at the cake before she blows out the candle. He looked at her telling her, "This cake is fit for a King but it's beautiful enough for my Queen, happy birthday baby."

Marilyn then blew out the candles with one long hard blow. Terry and Matthew gave her kisses. All of the loved ones were there. Marilyn couldn't believe what had happened. She was like, "What!" She couldn't believe she was conned like that. She thought about Aunt Helen, she knew there was something different about her, but she couldn't put her finger on it. Everyone was laughing. Terry handed Marilyn a glass of champagne and they held up their glasses and said, "forever young."

Everyone started conversing, then the children were taken to another part of the house where they could play, eat, and relax with each other. Ray Smith was a tall and slim young man who was responsible for keeping the music lively and that he did. Ray played a song especially for the birthday girl, 'Love is Many Splendid Thing.'

Terry took Marilyn's hand and held her ever so gently in his arms. Marilyn whispered in his ear, "Terry Hardy I love you for all of the things that you are not. You make my world go around, and around again and again. You put me on repeat."

Terry knew that was just the champagne talking, but he wanted her to know that later she will see what Terry is doing to her. She told him "O.K, you're the boss." They danced into the night with pictures being taken with plenty of champagne and delicious food.

Finally, Annie Marie Case, Marilyn's sister, got a chance to hug her. Annie gave her a hug and let her know that a hug is not the only thing she has for her. Annie reached under the table and pulled out a present and said, "Happy Birthday Sister," and they embraced each other.

Others were bringing out their gifts and Marilyn was so overjoyed, at this moment she felt like a queen on her throne. Marilyn felt like royalty, and she will never forget this moment, as she released her sister.

Aunt Helen walked over to Terry to say you did a "Good job son," Then she patted him on his back. "You really caught her off guard this time."

Terry knew she would be expecting something for next weekend which really is her birthday.
Aunt Helen started laughing and Terry joined in with her. "Keep it up son, it doesn't get any better than this."

Terry wanted to know, "Why not, is there an end, Aunt Helen?"

Aunt Helen gave him a huge hug with a smile to match with her approval.

It had gotten late, and couples had sectioned off to themselves. Everyone was in a mellow mood, setting around conversing. The card players had been playing for hours steadily. It was around 1:00 a.m. when everybody started departing. Helen reminded all of the parents not to forget their children while they're leaving.

"We will try not to." Someone replied.

All you could hear was a happy birthday and good night Marilyn, we love you. Terry and the family spent the rest of the night at Aunt Helen's. She loved that a lot.

It was 8:11 a.m. Sunday, the rain was falling, and the smell of bacon was the reason for Terry to open his eyes. Terry looked over beside him, all he could see was loveliness. He couldn't resist kissing her and Terry kept on kissing her until he reached her neck then he reached her shoulder and she never moved. Terry looked up at her face, Marilyn didn't open her eyes right away, but she had this warm smile. Terry was waiting for some kind of sign that she was awake. Marilyn began speaking clearly, "You know honey I was dreaming and there was this hot guy…"

Then Terry put his finger on her lips, "Yes, baby I know because I am that hot guy."

She responded "Well, this is your wife speaking, and you better not forget it, Your Hotness."

They spent more time together before eating breakfast, everything was just right. An hour later, they were dressed and ready for any kind of food. Matthew wasn't in his room and as they were approaching the kitchen, they could hear Matthew and Aunt Helen laughing and talking. Matthew and Helen were at the table eating breakfast.

Now they know why Matthew never intruded into their room, they both walked over and gave Matthew a kiss on his cheek. At the same time, Marilyn kissed the cheek on his left side while Terry kissed the cheek on the right. Everyone said good morning and Terry gave Helen a hug as they joined them for breakfast. Marilyn and Matthew were elated as they spent the rest of the day with their aunt, who was the best aunt in the world to Matthew.

Later, Matthew gave his all as he played kickball with his dad, falling over each other as they were trying to kick the ball. Aunt Helen and Marilyn had front row seats on the porch cheering them on. Aunt Helen watched Matthew playing kickball and to her surprise, Matthew played like a pro. Aunt Helen told Marilyn that Matthew is a fine child. "One day right before your eyes he will be all grown up but, in the meantime, I just know you'll enjoy that young man to the fullest. He is such a bright young man too."

Marilyn told her aunt that Matthew surprises her every day, but the funniest side of this scenario is before she became pregnant, she felt like something was missing in her life as she grew older. She felt empty when she saw other women with their children. When she got married and became pregnant, she knew it was right. During that period, she felt serene, and it has been that way ever since. While she was carrying him, she knew that was the missing piece of the puzzle and it didn't matter what sex it happened to be. Her newborn child was going to be loved.

The number one concern of hers was that her unborn child was healthy. That was her main concern, she told Aunt Helen. That alone would have driven her crazy.

Aunt Helen knew that her hair would have stood up on her head, but she just knew that wouldn't happen. "Being in that situation and a first-time mother would cause much stress for any mother to endure but thank God you didn't have to go through that challenge because you would have had to handle it. We would have given you all the love you needed. Darling, it shows your son how much you appreciate his existence."

As they clapped for Matthew scoring another point, Marilyn shouted, "That was a good one Matthew."

Aunt Helen mentions, "The way Matthew acts, his attitude, and the way he can hold a conversation. His demeanor shows me the assumption of what his parents are like."

"Wow! Aunt Helen, what a wonderful thing to say and you said it with such flow and ease, I couldn't have said it better myself."

Helen laughed as she leaned her head back. She didn't care about anything right then, except for Marilyn and her family. It didn't matter what they did because this moment was magical for her. They tried to talk about everything and everyone as well as they shared their own feelings for each other.

After they finished supper, Marilyn gave her aunt a huge hug. Marilyn thanked her for her awesome hospitality and for being a loving aunt. Terry and Matthew's feelings were mutual, which made it difficult to depart from Aunt Helen. Marilyn couldn't thank her enough. Marilyn thought of the appropriate words to say to her. She stated, "Aunt Helen, your feelings are genuine. You show that genuine love. Your love is so vital it is transferred from you to us."

Helen thanked all of them for their kind words and for a great visit. Afterwards the family started out on the road back home safe and sound.

Chapter 3
The Selected Events

Monday morning, around 9:00, Terry was at the South Side Meat Market to make sure everything was going on perfectly. Well, mainly because he was letting his right hand man, Lawrence Smith, take the lead for today. Lawrence didn't have any problem with Terry not being there, he felt that it was well deserved. Before Terry could leave, Mark had entered the market. Terry poured up two cups of coffee and handed one of the cups to Mark. Mark started off talking about the surprise birthday party. "How fascinating and so pleasant," He stated. That's all he had to say, not that he had to say anything else.

Mark didn't want to interrupt Terry's morning business traffic, because he knew there would be plenty of it and early. All in all, Terry assumed there was something going on with Mark. Before Mark could open his mouth to say anything else, Terry intervened. Terry reminded Mark, "If there's anything that you think you need, and I have it, then you got it."

Mark made it clear that he already knows who got his

back and, "…the same stands for you to my friend. Mark took a sip of his coffee, then set it on the bar. Terry explained that he's taken today off, "…and you caught me right as I was leaving. Your timing is great by the way."

Mark agreed his timing had always broken hearts. Then they chuckled, Mark told Terry this past weekend had several pretty low situations going on. They all took place in Hazlehurst Mississippi. The trouble started Thursday night actually. "My cousin in Hazlehurst explained, when the wife of a local telephone man reported to her husband that C. C. Baker, a twenty-eight-year-old Negro farmer, had spoken to her insultingly. As he moved towards her, she called her husband and he drove the Negro away with a pair of pliers. After that, the Posses were out searching for C. C. Baker but there was no trace of him to be found."

Terry looked at Mark, tilted his head, and said nothing. Mark continued by saying, "Well this story is not over yet. While feelings were still tense, Saturday afternoon, there was a lady named Mrs. Cydnee Hayes and a baby. They were run down by an automobile driven by a Negro girl. Both were seriously injured, and the accident precipitated the expulsion. A group of citizens hastily assembled, my cousin said they passed from house to house driving the Negroes before them down the streets to the city limits. Restaurants, business, and houses were cleared of blacks and driven cowering before the crowd with threats and blows. My cousin said no shots were fired, but the enraged citizens mobilized and using fists, clubs, and bricks, drove every Negro out of the town and forced them to stay outside the city limits. There was no resistance offered, my cousin said, and no further trouble was anticipated. This story ended with the city Marshall not able to recognize any of the members of the crowd."

Then Mark looked at Terry, he was still looking the same as before. Terry still didn't know what to say. Now Terry is acting like Mark was when he first entered the meat market. Now he knows why Mark wasn't acting normal. Terry had become numb about the whole situation because this has repercussions, just from hearing about the situation. He wondered what would happen if the Marshall did recognize anyone within a crowd? He knew the answer right away no one would recognize anyone, ever. That would be an excellent question under different circumstances.

Mark was being realistic about the situation. He knew Negroes really don't have a chance and he described it as being like "unwanted piss in a shoe." Terry looked at Mark then he laughed out loud. Mark has that effect on people and Terry let him know that he certainly has a way with words. Mark didn't hesitate to thank Terry for that comment because he knew only Terry would appreciate the talent. Terry could think of nothing but how crazy Mark was, but he was definitely glad that a mess like that didn't happen in their hometown. Mark knows that once that chaos sat in, it was a catastrophe to the end. Nothing good comes from that kind of behavior.

Everyone noticed that certain kinds of stories always raised eyebrows. Terry has the insight to know, it's just not enough eyebrows being raised to sort of speak. If there were enough it still would get out of control because of the way some people think. Sometimes, people can be too outrageous.

Well, Mark had forgotten about Terry's intention to leave. After he had commemorated then he reacted. "I think I need to be getting out of here before I persuade you into going somewhere with me and we end up gone all day."

By now, Terry was ready to move farther, reminding Mark to stop reading the newspaper. Those stories are wild, man. Mark, thank them for the coffee, then he sat the cup on the bar and they both headed toward the door. Mark reminded Terry that the meeting was still on for tomorrow and that he would pick him up. Terry strolled home after hearing this story that was unforgettable in the worst way.

Quietness was the key word for today. Quietness and romance because they had to make up for a lot of caring. That's exactly what Terry and Marilyn did Monday, all day long. It was a great plan, and it was just what the doctor ordered or what Terry ordered, that is.

It was Tuesday Feb. 22, 1927, when Mark called Terry to tell him that he was on his way to pick him up for the Ku, Klux, Klan meeting. It was wet outside because it had rained. Mark couldn't help but to notice the clouds as he was driving. They reminded him of his mother telling him about the clouds. She would say, "Look up at the sky. I promise you, there would be a portion of the clouds dipping out from the clouds downward toward the earth. That is called rain clouds and if you didn't know, you would have never noticed that it ever existed."

Mark thought it's so simple, so crazy and so amazing. God does work in mysterious ways. He thought, as he was about to reach one of his destinations. Terry was ready and like Mark, Terry was somewhat curious to know how people act at a meeting of this sort.

Terry told his wife that they shouldn't take long getting back, to just keep being my girl. As he got closer to her, he said, "And you're smelling too sweet," as he embraced her. No sooner than those sweet words were spoken, Mark drove up in the driveway. Terry gave Marilyn a kiss and headed out the door. He turned around and whispered, "I'll be back."

Mark was waiting for Terry in the truck, he spoke to Marilyn who was standing in the doorway. When Terry got into the truck, Mark looked over at Terry and whispered, "Sure you'll be right back. Let me tell you something that is real and funny. When have we gone anywhere and come right back or what's better than the last time we spent time together?"

Terry thought for a second and his mind went blank, "You can't be serious, it's been too long to be trying to figure it out." But Mark figured it was time to get out and about. He just likes to take a little time to get out every once and a while.

"You know it's good for the marriage to have some space in there for yourself and you know, that works for the entire family too. We all take time out for ourselves so we can grow to be our true selves in this world and just like I'm looking forward to this being a meaningful occasion. I believe in life we play many roles, sometimes time is good and sometimes they're fucked up." Mark didn't have any complaints because he was happy to have his friend spending this day in the midst of it all. Mark remembered the newspaper stating if it didn't rain the meeting would be held behind the Post Office, now because of the rain it will be held at the High School Auditorium. "To the high school auditorium, here we come."

Terry was excited as they got closer to their destination, he didn't realize that it had an impression on him. Mark has known Terry long enough to know that he's a curious person especially when it concerns something relating to searching a matter as this. Well, they have talked themselves all the way there. Now they will see what's really happening.

As they made an entrance, there were plenty of people there, to their surprise some of the people they knew. They were looking from the left to the right as they passed down several aisles before they took a seat. The meeting was all about the newly picked Grand Dragon of the Ku, Klux, Klan, of the Realm of Mississippi. His name was Howard A. Jackson, who was a native of Texas, a Lawyer by profession.

He served as First Lieutenant of the Great War and

was actively and prominently associated in church and fraternal affairs prior to becoming associated with the national movement of the Klan. He has held offices in all of the York Rite Bodies of Masonry and served two years as Worthy Patron of his home chapter of the Eastern Star. He is a deep student of History and Sociology and discusses national and social problems with a deep understanding of their importance to the nation. It ended saying, the Klan in Mississippi, chose Mr. Jackson as a Grand Dragon three months ago. The men weren't very talkative as they exited the building. On their way home, Mark was saying how, "Mr. Jackson, the Grand Dragon acted as Imperial Representative of the realm between the resignation of Mr. Watt in September and on the 15th of November 1926. He announced he was unanimously chosen. So, they thought well of him, do you have to accomplish all of that knowledge, to end up doing something so evil? They act as if their movement were more important than the President of the United States. After all, how intelligent do you have to be, to annihilate people's lives?"

Terry was confused because he thought when you're educated or through education, you're in a position to make concrete and intelligent decisions. If this is the result of being educated, then something went catastrophically wrong somewhere. Terry thanked Mark for suggesting him to come. Mark notices Terry seemed different after having attended the meeting and he likes adventuring in the unknown. There's a world of its own out there. That has made their life seem clearer but definitely an eye opener, meaning that there is a lot of trouble in the world. "That's because of Mr. Howard Jackson's background, the Ku Klux Klan are positioned in huge and small corporations everywhere. That's some kind of weight to be carrying around every day," Mark admitted.

Terry didn't like that, so he corrected him. "You mean some kind of hatred for people to be carrying around, don't you Mark. They can't see anything else beyond that. It would be hard for me to walk a straight line living that lifestyle but so many do and that's what saddens me. I really had a chance to actually see not one but multiple faces that's a part of our mankind and they were representing that kind of topic. Mark, I know this is the first time for you also."

"Yeah, you're right it felt good to be able to participate but scary all wrapped in one bundle, Terry man!"

Mark was about halfway to Terry's house, when he suggested that they should seek a restaurant because the Ku Klux Klan's meeting left him starving, "So how about it; before we call it a day?

"Mark, you are a mind reader too and with that said food can make it right, Amen," said Terry.

"Right now, I feel like you're a mind reader, you know, you can get paid for that." Mark replied. "You are funny Terry and you got jokes too, I know we need to be getting something to eat right now!" Mark finished.

Terry agreed, "That food will set the tone," it always

worked for him. The scenery will be great to mellow out because they were a little uptight.

After arriving downtown at Restaurant Fancy, it wasn't long before the men were sitting down at the table eating their meals that were well enjoyed and appreciated. Terry told Mark they have been friends for a long time. He paused for a second, then without hesitating, he told him, "For now on, we are like brothers. That's right, we are family."

"We are the only ones in our class who are still friends," Mark stated.

"Mark, your words are very touching, but I don't have any room to cry right now because this food is exquisite! It's fulfilling my greatest desire which means it's actually executed the plan it was meant to."

They both laughed. After the wonderful food, the two decided to explore some of their old territory, where they had periodically hung out. They were hoping and counting on seeing a familiar face since they haven't been there for a couple of years. It took about forty minutes to reach their destination going south.

The ride getting there turned out to be much more than they expected because the boys were all there. Now this was a reunion at a bar called The Place and the owner was truly pleased to see his favorite crowd all together again, having fun just because, the hell they could. Terry paid for a round of drinks, for the men, which were a round for four in all. While everyone was conversing with one another, Thomas Pain and Teddy E. Smith were sitting at a table, (a couple of their friends.)

Teddy Smith suggested to Mark, to take a stand, so they could listen to some of his new tunes. Mark did just that, he stepped up on the stage and he took that harmonica out of his pocket and began to play something that sounded like jazz. That sound was like no other as he played with his heart; he and his harmonica. His eyes were completely closed as his body moved slowly in a motion. The strangest things would happen when he played, one would feel a sense of release and calmness within. Mark knows how to make a person feel like a million bucks. When he started playing, it felt like everything was perfect and right then, it was. People were cheering Mark on as they gave him a warm applause as he brought it to a close.

Then someone else decided to step onto the stage, a young man who started telling some awesome jokes that helped make the time clock pass faster than the fun time clock, which is what closed The Place. Now it was time to say good night and to depart from friends, and they agreed to take care until the next time. They couldn't think of anything or anywhere else to vanish. They concluded, to say the least, that they weren't suitable enough to make another trip, so they were on their way home laughing and talking all the way.

After a long, hard sleep, Terry was surprised that he felt pretty civilized the next day. He felt about the same as he did when he stayed at home. Terry enjoyed himself that much at home, but he loved the variety also of meeting and being around people. That moment of it all is what keeps him going. It's like an adrenaline to him within itself. He decided to go into the meat market an hour later. He was with his wife a little longer, which was something he did as if it was a duty. He was doing it truly from his heart, unconditionally.

Around 7:30 a.m. Marilyn had to take Matthew to school so she was ready and making sure that he was ready so they could leave. On the way to school, Marilyn would call out number problems to Matthew. He knows his math, well his addiction and subtraction no one can take any money from him, she thought as she smiled. She loved his expressions. His eyes would get big and bright, and his lips would form into this wonderful smile. He would be so excited when he got it right, then he would say, "Yes!"

Marilyn took him to his school, Harris Elementary and gave him a huge hug and he took a seat like a little man. She would wave good-bye. Marilyn made it back home and Terry was still there. As soon as Marilyn made it inside their home, there stood Terry. She was surprised to see him there and next she asked if he was going to stay, "my love?"

Terry just took her hand without saying a word and led her to a chair in the kitchen where she sat. Then he spoke with the words, "I was waiting for you of course." Terry started talking to Marilyn with passion and excitement as he proceeded. Marilyn reacted enthusiastically as she listened to Terry. She did it with pleasure listening very closely, as he began telling her what had happened last night. Terry was sitting at the table in front of Marilyn and all he could see were her hazel eyes as well as her hair that was bright as the sun with curls that twisted and hung in her face and down her shoulder. As she smiled, her lips were a pale pink that matched perfectly with her cheeks, he thought.

Terry stayed on the subject of what had happened, but it wasn't easy, for she was breathtaking and that's all he could think of at that moment and the feeling was mutual. It was on, while sitting in the chair, that white blouse just seemed to slither down her shoulders. Terry started kissing her from her lips and slowly down her neck. Then he hit his favorite spot, Marilyn's boobs. Terry was so excited and that's when the clothes started flying everywhere. They didn't stop until every piece had floated to the floor. Terry placed her on the table. Marilyn danced for her husband as she moved her hips swiftly as they were so well put together. Marilyn placed her right thigh over Terry's left shoulder. Marilyn had all of Terry's attention. Then she moved her left thigh passionately over his other shoulder now she had Terry surrounded with the best. Terry took his time, moving slowly with her into his chamber.

It was a couple of hours later when Terry made it to work but he felt alright with that. One of his customers, who always came early, started teasing Terry for being awfully late this morning. He started chattering, "I was cheating with my wife, and everything was so right, I just felt like I was doing wrong.

Marilyn Hardy was her name and she felt like one of the most important people in the world to me."

His customers gave him great respect for his honesty and the love he shared with his wife as he went on with his day. That's how Terry Hardy really made her feel. She was sure of herself, and most women could sense that. She had something most women would kill to have, and she handled it, like a charm. It was easy for Marilyn because she knew what love felt like at its best, because she was living it.

Chapter 4
Binding Love

Marilyn has two sisters, Anne Marie Case, who is the oldest and Marilee Pain, the youngest. Marilee lives in Summit and she stays in touch with her sisters weekly. Marilyn decided to walk next door to visit her sister Anne Marie. She had to walk a little ways to get to the front door of her house. They're close in age, like a year apart. Normally, Marilyn visited her home anyway but today she decided to go unannounced to surprise her with her visit. No sooner than she knocked on the door, Anne greeted her with a "Good morning Marilyn," with open arms.

Marilyn was surprised at how fast she answered the door and she hugged her and said, "Good morning Anne, how about going jogging with an outgoing gal like me?"

Anne Marie expressed, "What! If you're trying to make every housewife in Brookhaven jealous, then O.k. you can count me in." Anne laughed as she welcomed her sister into her home. She fixed Marilyn a cup of hot chocolate to drink while she was getting ready. Marilyn didn't have any problem with that. Anne assumed Marilyn was there for her mean cup of hot chocolate, anyway.

Marilyn was sitting at the kitchen table when Anne sat a cup of hot chocolate in front of her. Marilyn thought the aroma was on a level of its own. "Hmm…" To smell it makes you think that you are tasting it. Then Anne told her to say nothing just taste, it speaks for itself. As she walked towards her bedroom she turned and looked at Marilyn to remind her that she'll be ready in a flash. Marilyn was sipping on her hot chocolate by then, and all Anne could hear was "Hmm, hmm.…"

Marilyn enjoyed going with her sister to get some exercise because of the privacy they had while they were jogging meant so much to her. They could jog until they passed out. Anne had enough land to make it happen. They both shared great walks, not to mention the scenery that Marilyn enjoyed the most along the way. There were plenty of beautiful trees with leaves of bright flashy colorful reds, yellows, and oranges during certain seasons of the year. Not to mention the peacocks that walked around like they owned the place. The peacocks alone would take your breath away. There were even large grasshoppers and butterflies with multiple colors on their wings. Marilyn speaks of it as if it were a scene straight out of a motion picture.

While they were walking, they would talk that stress out as well. Marilyn thought Anne would always have some interesting topic to converse about since she was single. From that thought, Marilyn mentioned to Anne that living the single life, she was looking good from where she was jogging. She knew Anne had something she would like to be freed from. But whatever it was Marilyn knew it was responsible for the weight that was obvious weighing heavily on her mind. But in a good way from the way she was smiling continentally.

Anne went from smiling to laughing because Marilyn had caught her off guard. But Marilyn nailed it right on the money. Now Anne didn't know what to say and she didn't know why she was keeping a secret. Then she came straightforward with the truth. Anne let her know that she had been dating a hunk of a man by the name of Charlie O'Brian.

Marilyn's mouth flew open, and the words flowed out, "What! Get out of here. You mean the Minister or is he a Deacon, let me think." Marilyn laughed and she told Anne, "You know that I know he's a Minister, sis." Anne Marie made it clear that he's a Minister, but they all represent the same cause, Amen. For what it's worth, he seems to be a pretty decent person.

Marilyn repeated the Amen to her sister, and I mean Amen. But she wanted her to understand that they all seem to be pretty decent people until you think you're in a real relationship with them. She explained, "No matter what he says, you will know more about him when you see him under pressure. When that happens, he will show his true color and you can determine from that reaction. If he comes through smelling like a rose, then he is one of the appropriate ones. Until then, he will have to prove me wrong. Not getting off the subject but we need to slow down for a minute. This jog took longer than I thought, or I really needed to work out."

Anne let Marilyn know that actually, they hadn't been jogging that long, particularly for an outgoing gal like herself. Well, they slowed their pace and going slow meant a lot to Marilyn. Then Marilyn looked at Anne and gave her a sad face then they came to a stop. Marilyn took a deep breath, she just inhaled then exhaled for a minute, until she rejuvenated enough to ask Anne to tell her more about Charlie O'Brian, for instance, has he ever been married before?

Anne Marie was touched by Marilyn's concern, and she let her know the answer was no. "He came close to that point, a year ago. We enjoyed being to ourselves, for instance, you know, going to various states. The people that we did mingle with are now acquaintances. We really like that very much. He's a handsome man, intelligent, his words have strength, and he has confidence. Most of all, he gives me plenty of attention and that alone is enough for me," Anne Marie stated, as they started walking, this time at a regular pace, instead of jogging.

After hearing Anne's remark, all Marilyn could say was, "Well now Miss Anne Marie."

Anne Marie believed in just telling it like she sees it. She explained how she came about this answer, and it was from listening to other women talking. They say it all the time that they needed someone in their life and one day, there he was. They knew he was the one. Just because a person flirts or says something nice to you doesn't mean you have to start turning that into a relationship. You will meet numerous men that will do the very same thing.

Marilyn listened to her sister and wanted to hear more. Now Marilyn wanted to know how this spark ignited. She knew her sister well enough to know that a relationship had to get started by a spark not lighting. Anne had her hair drawn back in a ponytail with sweat on her nose and forehead and looked at her sister because she was darn good. Anne revealed that she takes her time with men, to gain information of what's really on their mind. "I need direct cognition to what that person is all about because the appearance on the outside of that person may bear no resemblance to what's really going on inside. That can be difficult and extremely frightening too."

Marilyn agreed, she never thought about it that way. "You know it wouldn't hurt to just strike up a conversation every once and a while because you never know what would come from it."

Anne picked up a rock and threw it into the pond. She told Marilyn, she had made a promise that she would be kind to herself and would be her own best friend through the power of God. You could feel the strength in her words.

Marilyn yelled, "I know what you mean Anna!"

"Of course you do," Anne Marie explained to Marilyn.

"I know you do." Marilyn replied.

"We need to train ourselves, you know, by loving ourselves first. I would never allow anyone to treat me below the standard I have for myself." Anne Marie stated.

Marilyn understood her sister too well and told Anna, "You –are- talking- now! That makes more sense just hearing it flowing out of your mouth."

Anne suggested taking control over yourself, then you can handle situations in a more intelligent way. With that being said, Marilyn was reminded of how she is with her husband, but it's somewhat different, but maybe not, she thought. Marilyn said, "Terry works very hard, but he shows me love in many, awesome ways."

"Of course," explained Anne Marie, "Because the love you two have is unconditional. You guys have that capital T and that capital L, which means you have that True Love." Marilyn looked at her sister and thanked her from her heart. Then they stop walking to give in to the heartfelt moment with a warm embrace. Anne Marie reminded Marilyn, "There will be no crying after this hug."

"You know that's true sister. You know some people wonder if there's such a thing as true love and what does it feel like. But you know what I think, I think the question is, are some of us capable of loving?" She continued saying, "I think everyone does, but they may show their love differently. Some people love the only way they know how to love. Just think, what are the chances of finding someone that can love, in the way, you need to be loved? You know Marilyn, like that you have," Anne Marie stated. As they both laughed with joy.

Anne believed there's a reason for things that happen, and it plays an important role in itself, also. "You know sis, you could meet someone for the first time in your life and he or she could catch your eye right then at that moment and you know you had to see that person again. That person did all the right things that you loved from then on to please you and you were doing the same and loving it. He was getting to know you, doing just enough for you to miss him but not being overbearing. Would you call that love or lust?" Anne Marie asked.

Because of the caring they both shared, Marilyn told Anne, "Girl, you know me, I would call it love, definitely."

Anne assured her, there was no doubt, that's exactly what she's expecting or something close to it. You can believe me, when it happens, you will be the first to know. Marilyn believed she would do just that. Marilyn noticed that they were getting closer to the house and how the walk was an excellent work out that made her feel vigorous. Marilyn brought attention to what had happened in the Negroes neighborhood in Hazlehurst Mississippi. She addressed how glad she was about how the situation didn't get any crazier, because it could have, you know.

Anne Marie agreed she felt the same. "No one should have to go through such brutality and by you verbalizing it alone shows that it's a concerning matter. I wouldn't want to become involved in anything like that in my lifetime. For me, it's hard just mentioning it."

Marilyn didn't know what she could do but she knew

that there was cause for some immediate attention. That's some kind of inappropriate behavior, for sure. You can't help but to be concerned for people who are being picked on and being punished for something they don't even know anything about and that's for anyone.

Annie Marie felt depressed over the matter of concern. As she spoke to her sister, the tone of her voice had weakened. "Marilyn, it's hard anytime someone has the advantage over anything or in this case over anyone, there's a little hope for the disadvantage that's involved. It's a bad position to be in because whatever happens, there wouldn't be anything done about it. You're a victim for hell to the end! For me, this isn't the best topic to speak on, it contributes to bad feelings for me." They were on the steps at the door of Anne's home before they knew it, the walk was completed.

Come on in Marilyn, we'll relax a minute.

Marilyn asked, "Do you think Marilee will visit this Sunday?"

"Our sister would never miss a visit to be with us on Sundays and we always enjoy her visits," Anne replied.

"Hell yeah," said Marilyn. They went into the den and Marilyn flopped down in a chair, leaning back, with her arms stretched out and her legs spread apart. Anne Marie felt so energetic she stretched out across from Marilyn in a chair. They looked over at each other and laughed.

Marilyn changed her tune just a bit to Anne about being

energetic too. "I may not look energetic right now, but I am a person who is feeling very energetic. You can believe me or not, but please just let me be for a minute."

Anne Marie was still laughing as she managed to tell Marilyn, "Shut up! You always have me laughing and it hurts to laugh hard like this. You're so funny, I just love it when you visit, you're such a fool, girl.

Marilyn shouted, "You know it! I can do this all day, but I just don't have the time. But Anna, anytime you need laughing therapy just call me over, I got your back. Another thing, I know we had to walk at least two miles, didn't we?"

Anne Marie responded, "You know we did, and it was worth every aching step. If you like, you are welcome to the bathroom, be my guest."

So, Marilyn took her up on the bath and Anne Marie did the same. Anne enjoyed having the presence of her sister in her home. It was so beautiful she felt it as an imperative duty to entertain. It took thirty minutes to finish with their baths. To Marilyn's surprise, Anne had clothes laid out on the bed for her. Anne made sure her sister was comfortable and fully relaxed. Anne Marie stuck her head in the bedroom and suggested getting a bite to eat and Marilyn agreed. They both went into the kitchen together, while Marilyn gave hints on her outfit, of how good it fitted.

Anne Marie started putting food on the stove while Marilyn set the table for two. Marilyn offered her help, but

Anne had no problem preparing the food, she had everything under control. She said that Anne had a beautiful plate of bright, colorful, noodles dishes with garlic butter shrimp that were spicy hot and golden, brown rolls with two glasses of white wine. Marilyn thought, if it tasted half as good as it looked, she was going to have a hard time staying away from Anne's kitchen. Anne took a seat at the table and blessed the food. Now Marilyn had the chance to taste that first mouth full. She had her eyes closed as she chewed very slowly like it was her last meal. Anne laughed at Marilyn and reminded her if she didn't watch it, she'd be in the need to run every day. Of course, Marilyn let her know that she's got this, "Believe me, it just tastes so luscious."

Marilyn wasn't going to make herself feel guilty over this fine food, so she started back chewing it slowly to really enjoy it. She wanted Anne to know that this is the kind of reward you should receive from a long walk, a light and delicious one. She looked at Anne with those big brown eyes saying, "This is wonderful my sister. This could be served to the King of England my dear with no disappointment."

Anne loves the idea of her food being the main attraction. She knew her sister would be back for more walks because food does taste better when someone else cooks it. Never-the-less, Marilyn thanked her sister for the wonderful meal that they both shared together. There wasn't anything that could replace the time the two spent together. Marilyn insisted on doing the dishes after they finished but Anne had a better idea. She mentioned, if they both did the dishes, they would be finished in half the time. Actually, Marilyn didn't know what to think but she thought this would be interesting since they never got along when they were younger. Their friendship meant so much to her then but more so now. It's a very important part of her life because she knows that everyone needs their family, that togetherness and that means a lot to her.

All at once, Annie Marie was face to face with that skeleton that has been sitting in the closet. Now she knew this was her moment more than ever to take a stand and become a real big sister. She stared at Marilyn, for a minute then she said, "I know I have always given you an exceptionally hard time. I can't explain why I didn't see eye to eye with you, but I got it now. You see what washing dishes together can do for you."

Anne noticed that Marilyn had a smile on her face, the whole time. She was so thankful to be a part of that moment. Anne realized for the first time how troubled Marilyn had been for all of those years and the passing of their mother, five years ago, didn't help any. Anne told Marilyn that she knew it had to be hard, but she didn't realize how much she needed her, or they needed each other. Plus, "I was too irrational to realize that something was missing in my life also. You know Marilyn, it's easier to spot what is missing or what's wrong in someone else's life. You can totally overlook what is going on in your own life. I don't know why, but maybe we think we are doing the right things. Maybe- just maybe, if we paid more attention to what we are doing to each other, we wouldn't have such a fucked-up outcome, ourselves."

Marilyn was simply astonished to see how much they have accomplished via a great meal and washing the dishes. Marilyn was calling it a day to head home. "I need to check on my house, I know it's probably missing me by now from all of the chores that need to be done."

Anne Marie wasn't going to settle with remarks like, the house missing you. "Now let's go to some place where it's nice and easy. What about shopping, we could do that until the children get out of school."

Marilyn responded, "That sounds like a winner, I will call Terry and let him know what is going on, just in case we don't make it in time to pick up the kids."

As they were getting everything in order, Anne got the truck and drove it to the front of the house. Marilyn was all set and ready to go, she locked the front door, and they were on their way. The sisters just rode for a while in the direction of an area called Wesson. It's an area with lots of trees and a large lake that's called Lake Lincoln. The weather was cool, and the temperature was in the upper 60s, which means the weather was just right because southern climates when humid are no joke. The sisters ended up at Lake Lincoln enjoying the view and just inhaling the fresh air that seemed to smell so fresh and so clean.

Anne had a blanket in the back of her truck, and she

pulled it out so they could sit on it with a bottle of fine wine and two glasses, cheese, and crackers. They were there long enough to finish bonding by confessing what they were guilty of, all of their rights and wrongs. They had their revelation time of experiments. Things that were revealed to be true even a tear or two were shed. Marilyn was leaning back on her hands with the wind blowing through her blond wavy hair as the tears rolled down her face.

Anne Marie, who was never good at manifesting her feelings; she was trying to hold them back, but her emotions took over. As they both were deeply touched. Anne looked at her watch and noticed that they had enough time to not have to rush picking up the kids from school. She thought "how the time of the day gives her the impression of having wings and gliding off into the midair." But they were there long enough to accomplish their mission of pleasing a combination of elements in which they put together as a whole to form their harmony.

They picked up everything and put it back on the truck. Anne admitted she was a little tipsy, but she was not going to drive, and she knew Marilyn could handle it. Marilyn patted Anne on her back while she was getting into the car. Marilyn started the engine up then both of them burst into a hard laugher, and they were still laughing when they drove off. The conversation was great but only with the windows down. Anne had some gum and gave Marilyn a piece and Anne assured her that they needed it. Marilyn couldn't believe that they were two drunken heifers going into the school to pick up their kids. It wasn't long before Marilyn pulled into the school, and they managed to handle that matter with ease as Brandon and Matthew were surprised to see their mothers together.

They were safe and at home from what turned out to be a long and pleasant day for the ladies. Marilyn drove into her own driveway so Anne could drive her vehicle home. Marilyn reminded Anne of how remarkable she had made her day as she exited the vehicle. Marilyn mentioned that she had to get that ham ready for the oven, then to the table. "I know we didn't discuss the subject of you having dinner with us and Matthew would love the attention."

Anne Marie didn't want her to be mistaken, she wanted everything to be understood that she's no fool, she loved good food and the answer was, yes. "Well, since you own the meat market, I would think your home would be the best place then any. I know you love my house," as she snickered, "but we have the rest of our life to go from your home to mine. I will bring my guess and my son of course and you know I will bring a dish or two."

That sounded like a well thought out plan to Marilyn as she told Anne the time was set for, "1:00 p.m. tomorrow, we will meet. By then we will be well sober and ready for some more wine." Anne Marie knew everything would be perfect, as they terminated their talk and she proceeded home.

Hours later, when Terry entered his front door, there was this pleasant but serious smell that was leading him straight to the kitchen until he heard this small voice coming from the living room as he was passing by. When he looked in that direction, he saw his two favorite people. Marilyn was on the floor, coloring in the coloring book with Matthew. She was telling him a story; about a baby Polar Bear who was lost and looking for his mother and asking questions along the way.

He had a smile on his face as he headed to the bathroom to take a bath before anyone could see him plus, he was thinking, I'm the man. They were into what they were doing so they didn't notice that he had come in. While the water was getting ready, Terry started running fast into the living room, moaning loud and jumped down to the floor near them. Marilyn and Matthew's eyes bucked, and their mouths flew wide open. When Terry landed on the floor, he started rolling over and laughing. Then he stopped rolling and that was a sight to see. He was laughing and they started hitting and punching him. He turned over on his stomach then he noticed what they were coloring and asked them to wait a minute. Then he picked up one of the coloring sheets and stared at it mysteriously. There was something different about this one and Terry looked at Matthew, "whoever colored this one will receive something special one day!" Matthew looked at his dad with those hazel eyes, frizzy hair, and he claimed it. Terry hugged Matthew telling him, "This looks like you could be a famous painter, that is what I see son." Matthew's eyes bucked as he thanked his dad.

Terry started talking to his son telling him, "You can do and be whatever you want to be, as long as you remember to always do your best. When you give your best, that's all you can do. Try to always think positive and I promise, you will recall me saying, 'Whatever you do, always do your best.' I will be there with you always. Your Mother can draw, that's where you got your talent form. I would take the credit for it, but you might ask me to draw something, and I can't. Let me get in here and take a bath while you two finish your coloring."

Matthew yelled, "Hurry up daddy,"

Marilyn said, "Take all the time you need and then some, sweetie."

When Terry returned from taking his bath, they spent the rest of the day getting the feast together for the next day and just enjoying life.

Thursday February 24, 1927, at 7:15 a.m. Terry was still in the bed with his eyes closed. Then his eyelid twitches and his left lash parted and revealed the bluest set of eyes you ever seen as if you could see the ocean moving in them. He sat on the edge of the bed then he stretched into a stand and started getting ready for work. Marilyn was dressed and ready to take Matthew to school. Marilyn told him she had invited some family members for dinner.

Then Terry decided to work for a few hours and would

be headed home for the family gathering. Terry wanted Marilyn to know, it feels great or better yet, how great it is to wake up with the aroma of wonderful food! It makes you feel the sense of royalty. Babe, it has a heavenly feel about it, and you can surprise me as often as you like when it comes to food. Marilyn knew exactly what he was saying. Terry laughed as he put his arms around her, he whispered in her ear, I'll be back soon and when I do, I'll have the boys with me so worries less. This will be a beautiful day for all of us.

"Yes! That will be just right," Then Marilyn announced that his sister-in-law will be over also. "We'll have everything under control in the kitchen area and I'll inform her about you picking up the boys, o.k. She gave him a kiss on his lips and there was Matthew running through the door giving his dad a kiss. I'm going to take Matthew to school so I can finish tidying up the loose ends and I love you." Then they were out the door, mercifully they departed.

It was around 12:30 when Anne and her guests arrived. Marilyn had a chance to meet Rev. Charlie O'Brian for the first time, well, the first time knowing of him in a courting situation. Anne arrived with a colorful dish that finished that special touch for their fabulous meal.

Marilyn poured up several glasses of wine to drink so they would get in that relaxing mode. Rev. O'Brian was pleased with the warm hospitality that Marilyn presented. He thought she was just awesome as well and now he can have the chance to get to know her and her family. Within the next hour Terry entered the kitchen door, the house filled with excitement and laughter especially when the little people entered the home. The two boys were looking for their moms and they both gave hugs.

The boys acknowledge Rev. O'Brian, he admits the boys are good looking kids with great demeanor. "Well, thank you for being so kind Rev. O'Brian," from the mouth of Marilyn thanking him for saying such nice things.

Rev. O'Brian was overwhelmed to see well-mannered children. It reminded him that someone's paying attention to their children. He knew Brandon made him feel overwhelmed, now it's two of them, they made his day. Then he reached into his pocket pulling out a couple of dollar bills and he gave ones to each of the boys. That movement put a huge smile on the boys' faces and they thanked him. Terry walked in and introduced himself. Marilyn and Anne excused themselves so they could get the table set up to enjoy a wonderful meal. Marilyn told the boys to wash their hands first then take a seat at the table, in that order.

By 1:30p.m., everyone was sitting in position at the dining table, while Rev. Charlie O'Brian blessed the food. Food was being passed around and across the table with much laughter in the air. Rev. O'Brian started telling his story of how he came into the ministry. Now Terry, all he could think about was Rev. O'Brian. He was thinking that he seemed like a decent fellow for my sister -in -law but I need to meet with him a couple more times. Well, he's only been dating for a little while now. We'll see what comes of this.

Marilyn was thinking, "M-m-m, I wonder if he's putting on airs for us because he knows we're noticing every little thing he does. Yeah, he's in the spotlight alright. He knows, he would have to stay on his P's and Q's, and you never know who's wearing a robe these days." As she smiled nodding her head as to respond to what Rev. O'Brian was saying.

Everything went as smooth as a baby's behind. If there wasn't anything said, the table was beautifully, filled with delicious food. All that needed to happen was to enjoy and take things all in stride. A while later, the adults vacated the table, and everyone had a glass in their hand. Even the boys follow with their glasses also, to go relax in the Den. Before anyone could get seated Terry announced, let's make a toast and Terry did the honor. In a calm voice, Terry asked for all of them to have a continual moment of joy, peace, and happiness in their life until it overflows into full time. As they all held up their glasses, even the boys. Everyone said, "Here, here!" Then every glass clicked. Matthew and Brandon let their glasses tap twice and excused themselves from the Den. They had bigger fish to fry, playing with toy trains in the bedroom .

Terry asked the minister if he liked to play chess and the minister's reaction was "bring it on!" In the meanwhile, Anne Marie and Marilyn listen to music with a glass of wine as they conversed. Anne Marie was so pleased with her sister Marilyn and now she had the chance to tell her that, "She could not have said it to a more caring or nicer person than me," your little sister Marilyn.

Anne heard how she felt as they were sitting. She placed her glass of wine on a table near her. Anne Marie asked Marilyn to look at her, "Do you know how brilliant you are? You came up with this idea for all of us to meet today and it was an unselfish one to be thankful for and I love you for making it possible. You know that's how you are; you have that caring touch added to it and you did it so cleverly by not telling me directly."

"Well, my sister Anne, I must say, those words are beautiful," said Marilyn. Anne Marie couldn't help but to laugh as Marilyn joined in.

After a couple of games of chess, Rev. O'Brian felt right at home and told Marilyn just that. "What a day, I must say, it was a pleasure being in your family's presence and the meal was excellent," as he thanked her. Anne Marie went to get Brandon and to let Matthew know that they were about to leave.

While Anne was getting Brandon, Marilyn and Terry were thanking Rev. O'Brian for gracing their home with his presence. Marilyn let him know that he's welcome to their home, and they enjoyed him as well. "We will be looking forward to seeing you again." Terry recommended that he come back soon and try to win in another game of chess. Anne Marie was back with Brandon as they all embraced each other but Brandon hated to leave as they went out of the door.

Friday morning Terry entered the meat market with a smile on his face, knowing that his staff was already there, getting the meats ready for another propitious day. To his surprise an old friend entered the meat market. Enthusiastic was Terry's response because he never would have thought his friend Thomas Pain would show up visiting someone. Yet, there he stood, and Terry greeted him with a handshake, then a hug. Terry began to tell Thomas how he never visits and asked him was everything alright? Thomas Pain just told it like it was, and that meant the way he saw it. "I found myself driving and here I am. As you know, I could have ended up in a place with a great amount of alcohol surrounding my mouth making it very happy."

Terry started choking after he heard that. Then he started rambling, saying, "You certainly could have been a comedian. But the reality of it was I knew you were not lying about the alcohol part." He couldn't believe he had chosen visiting him over drinking but maybe there is a new man being born again in that tough skin. If any of that was so, that would make him a hell of a man.

Thomas admits it to be, "All true and I am here. You were on my mind, and I followed it through to find you healthy and working, that all that matters to me right now man. I'm not staying long, I just needed to get out and be effective today. I have accomplished that already." He took a deep breath then he exhaled declaring that he had always had things to do, that he didn't want to do. "I guess I'm like everybody else when I want to do something I feel like I should do just that."

Terry was nodding his head in agreement. He looked at Thomas and smiled, "You know man, that's just like us having to take the bitter with the sweet. There are times when that darn bitter seems to outweigh that sweet, but we have to keep moving on because that's what we do. After all, nobody wants a broke ass man."

Thomas agreed that is like being called a bitch. "Man, because that's what it makes you feel like, that you are looking like you are on that bitch level. That's not a good feeling, you know the money would have to keep flowing."

"I'm Terry Hardy and that is exactly what I'm talking about."

As they started walking towards the door, they ended up taking the conversation on the outside. Terry still couldn't believe Thomas had actually thought about him, he felt elated. He knew for someone to think about you, then that someone visited you, he thought, now that's awesome. Thomas didn't want to keep Terry from his business, so he brought the conversation to a close by shaking Terry's hand and he drove off. Terry kept that good spirit for the rest of that day, and it was all brought on due to Thomas Pain's visit.

Chapter 5
The Visitors

During this time period, there were some of the Black families who didn't have a place that they could call a home of their own. These people or families survived by living on other people's land. In the process of not having their own land, they had to work the lands of these people in order to pay for personal items that they needed to survive.

Thomas Pain was one of Terry Hardy's drinking buddies, brother –in -law and dear friend, who lived in Summit. Thomas' wife was Marilee Pain and his five years old son Jeremiah Pain. Thomas was a complicated man whose home was surrounded with people. One of the Black families that farmed his land was the Haynes Family.

Saturday morning Thomas Pain awakened and stimulated early to make a run to the stores like he always did. He would buy what everyone needed so he always kept his transportation in good running order. After all, he had no chores but to enjoy going shopping. Thomas would drive to Pike County and all you would see were horses hitched to buggies and T-Motor Cars, were all over the place. Then like magic Thomas would be in the mix of it all. He noticed people all around doing something in common, getting things that they needed and at the same time people were making that connection with one another. That was the most pleasing behavior part of it all.

As he saw a couple of friends that he hadn't seen for over a year. Thomas asks himself, "How large is this town and where do these people be, most of the time? Thomas thought, "The feeling you have from just meeting people is like therapy to the soul."

Thomas finished shopping for all of the items on his list and he headed home. As soon as he returned, all of the families were happy to see that he had arrived.

The mother of the Black family was named Alma Haynes. Alma was a sweet, five feet and two inches in height, with smooth caramel skin and blue eyes. Her long black wavy hair hung halfway down her back. She would wear it in two huge braids, most of the time to assist its maintenance. Alma looked like a full, blooded Indian. She was part Cherokee and Black, it was beautiful on her.

Alma and Ralph Haynes had five children to care for while living on Thomas Pain land. Their family consisted of three girls, Hazel, Mandy, and Annie Bell was the youngest. Their sons were named Leo and Curtis. Alma was waiting to receive their groceries that Thomas Pain had picked up at the store. Thomas called out the name and they would receive their items. When Thomas didn't have anything left to give, Alma was astonished because of their circumstance they had needs for their kids also. Alma didn't hesitate in responding to Thomas as to why he didn't purchase the groceries.

To Thomas' knowledge he couldn't recall being asked to bring anything. Alma looked at Thomas and all was on her mind was, he didn't bring anything for us. She deeply expressed to Thomas that he knew to bring something for their kids. Alma left feeling indignant as she walked through a short pass to tell her husband.

It didn't take long before Ralph was walking over to Thomas while yelling, "What in the hell were you thinking about not bringing any items?"

Ralph stood there waiting for an answer while Thomas looked at Ralph and leaned forward yelling, "You just go and get the wagon and get to work."

Ralph did just that, he got the wagon hooked up to the horse. He took a set in the wagon and laid his gun on his lap. When Thomas saw Ralph with a gun on his lap, he started running and jumped in his car and skidded off on two tires. Thomas eventually returned, with plenty of groceries. Everything turned out for the better, and peace returned.

The Haynes Family farmed Thomas Pain's land, among a few other families. The men and women worked as Sharecroppers during the spring and summer months. The men cultivated the land by plowing the soil. You would see the long even rolls that looked perfect. The sharecroppers were divided into sections, working together in order to make the job move easier. There were small holes made by certain workers of the sharecroppers where the seeds were to be placed. As the seeds were placed a small amount of dirt covered them. In order for the seeds to grow, there was plenty of water and a lot of caring. The grass would grow like wildflowers, so in order for the crops to grow healthy, they had to work regularly to keep it manageable.

The women would start working the farm early in the morning. By noon, they would finish their chores to take care of their children and to prepare their meal. As the crops grew, there was cotton, corn, sugar cane and potatoes. Many of the men wore hats and the women wore scarves to help block the sun as they moved about, attending the crops. The crops are worked and harvested as the crops ripen. Then they are prepared for customers to purchase. The process is continued until the end of the crop's season. When the family brought forward what they had harvested, Thomas would add up what each family or person shared. Then Thomas deducted some of what was owed to him, each time from what they made.

Ralph Haynes did pretty much what he wanted to do. He was tall and a very slim man. Ralph stood six feet and three inches tall. He looked even taller because he was a slim man. He also had smooth, dark skin that was very noticeable and that was mainly because he's a combination of Black Water Creek Indian and Black. Ralph did what he had to do when it came to his family and that was to make things happen. He accomplished what they needed and most of the time that wasn't easy.

Ralph wanted to take his family away from that place, but he knew the end results would be the same. So those feelings were repressed for now. He knew many people, and many knew him as well. By working, keeping up with everything the family needed, Ralph didn't have the energy to move around as much as he would have liked. It was extremely hot working directly in the sun which contributed to his low energy. But he managed to get around, after all, he couldn't let that stop him.

It was a beautiful Saturday, July 2, 1927, it never looked so good, and it was so hot. Ralph went to one of his friend's houses, and they would sit and talk. Norman Harrison was his name and his friends enjoyed stopping by often to spend time just talking and having a drink or two.

Norman asked Ralph about Alma and the kids and that he knew the kids were keeping him strong. Ralph agreed they are growing up so fast man sometimes you want to ask, "Who are these children? If they were gone for a while, well that would be hard. All and all I love them and that's how it is and thank you for asking."

Norman looked at Ralph and said, "I know you love them, that's all day every day. Marilee Pain is she still putting up with that old husband of hers? I wouldn't be surprised if she just rode off into the sunset, putting up with Pain. But she must love him somehow, I guess."

Ralph smiles saying, "You know Marilee and Thomas got to love each other but they are quite a pair. There's always something going on and that's for sure. We all do what we have too. You know things would get corrupted around there, like really quickly."

Norman knew how Thomas Pain could become a pain in the ass and that's what it sounded like was happening now. "You know Ralph," shaking his head, "Thomas is a good man," then he laughed. "The thing is he just didn't like having to take shit off of anyone. He would like to be in control, huh." All Ralph could say was between my dad and Pain, Ralph couldn't say anything else. Ralph just hung his head down and shook it. Norman thought for a minute, "You know Ralph, as a matter of fact your dad is a good man. It's just that he doesn't take shit off of anyone. I bet you he didn't take shit off of his mama either. Norman laughed so hard thinking he was so funny. They sat on the front porch in a couple of chairs. Norman brought two shot glasses and two glasses of water and a bottle of whiskey. Norman poured whiskey in two of the glasses and handed one to Ralph. Ralph took a sip and said, "Wow! Did you brew this yourself because man this is an eye opener literally, my eyes are just staying wide open?"

Norman laughed, "No man but it's good, isn't it?"

"I must say Harrison, it's good and you always manage to keep it like that. Ralph started a conversation about his father,

Virgil Haynes. How his dad left Thomas Pain home about two months ago. "You know for yourself how much love they had for each other, and he showed no emotion when he spoke. Pain wasn't in a good mood at all that day. You move right along trying to ignore him but he's too damn good at that game. My dad was hooking up the plough so he could start working. Pain was standing off from him saying, 'too slow about doing every damn thing, good for nothing Nigger.' Just as Pain spoke those words daddy started taking the single tree off of the plough. Pain was walking off when he said, 'Now you don't want to do anything stupid, and you haven't even started yet.' When Pain finished that sentence daddy had successfully taken the single tree off the plough. Then Pain slowly turned around and that's when daddy started whipping Pain with that single tree; yelling and whipping him like he was a child." Norman had just put a shot of whiskey in his mouth when it came spraying back out of his mouth. Ralph said, "When dad finished whipping Pain he ran off into the woods." Harrison couldn't stop laughing and asked Ralph to give him a minute to breathe.

Ralph then continued by saying, "Pain had an ass whipping like he never had before. Everyone who had witnessed what had happened was forever delighted. They didn't think they would see something so funny happening to Mr. Pain. Mr. Pain didn't think it was funny worth-a-dame. Before long, the Sheriff and a Deputy drove up. Marilee and others showed the Sheriff where daddy started running among the woods so they could start tracking him in the right direction. The Sheriff never attempted to go into the woods to capture daddy. After sitting around for a while, they had decided to leave. They know Virgil was a mean man, and they knew it could take a while getting him out of those woods. The Sheriff reminded Pain if he needed their services again, they would be glad to help and they drove off. Hours later Virgil reappeared, gathering a few clothes, and headed to New Orleans. While Pain, to a certain degree, was certainly uncomfortable getting to sleep that night. Pain behavior was different for a short period. During that short period there was a bit of peace."

Norman was ecstatic with what he had heard. Ralph really had him by his ears this time. He thanked Ralph for being responsible for making a man's day. "I haven't heard anything quite so funny in a while. I almost forgot how good it felt not just to laugh but to laugh with all my might."

Ralph clarified that he did just that and "you were laughing so hard I started laughing from watching you laugh."

Norman mentioned to Ralph about this thirty-year-old Black male, who worked as a farm laborer, and he wanted to know if he heard of a man by the name of Shug Caffie? Ralph didn't have a clue to who this person was, but he knew he sounded like someone who was sorry.

Norman scratched his head and poured up another shot of whiskey as it touched his lips. It flowed down his throat followed by some cool water. Then he spoke about Shug Caffie doing a great deal of sorry things, to say the least. "Man, I know you don't hear a damned thing about anything so you need to be coming by here to visit more often, so I can keep you up to date with the news." Ralph smiled as he listened.

Ralph got stuck looking at Norman's shiny bald head and his pointed nose as he was making a point saying how Sheriff Taylor had been seeking Shug Caffie for over a week now. "They are without a clue where he could be hiding. You know somebody is hiding him somewhere."
Ralph reminded him that the person he's talking about sounds like his dad, especially the part about being hard to keep up with.

Norman turned his head quickly in Ralph's direction and said, "Yeah, you are right about your dad." Mr. Haynes is one of a kind, but Shug Caffie was a different situation totally. He was recognized coming out of Mr. Duke's house and he wasn't a guest."

"What? You mean a black man sneaked into a white man's house? That sounds like suicide, that's crazy. I know of Mr. Duke, he's a well-known farmer." Ralph said as he swallowed down a shot of whiskey and leaned back in his chair.

Norman asked Ralph to wait a minute as he was just getting started. "What you need to know is that Shug was in Duke's daughter's bedroom. I don't know how old his daughter was, but I know she was young. Shug was discovered in the girl's room. He was able to escape but in the process of doing that, he was recognized. All I know, he was wearing a tar mask covering the lower part of his face."

Ralph knew whoever saw him had to have known him well to identify him while he was running with a roughly made mask on his face.

Norman Harrison agreed, "How true and it happened in the northeast part of Amite County in the Thompson neighborhood. The sheriff, N. P. Taylor had been searching for Shug for a week now. Then he finally got some relief. He received a tip that Shug was on a farm in the neighborhood of Summit last Sunday. That Sheriff Taylor was also looking for another black man, who killed someone last Saturday. Deputy Blunder was responsible for Summit area, so Sheriff Taylor asked Deputy Blunder to run the Negro down." Harrison continued, saying, "That Shug Caffie record was bad, he was convicted at the last term of court for attacking a black girl and he was arrested and given a prison sentence. Just recently Shug completed his term and feelings against him ran high ever since the attempted attack was reported. There were white men who had grouped off in parties and had been searching quietly for Shug. The parties were bent on vengeance, but Deputy Blunder arrested Shug Caffie at 1:00 a.m. Thursday morning. Blunder placed him in jail in Summit, but within minutes, he realized that the jail was too insecure in case of an attempt at violence."

Ralph was trying to keep a good feeling by keeping his whiskey flowing, he took another sip. He was listening, hardly blinking an eye. Norman refilled their glasses of water to drink with their whiskey. Then he continued, "Deputy Blunder took Shug out of jail and headed to Magnolia where he could be held in the Pike County jail for his safety. Deputy Blunder got to a telephone as quickly as possible and the Sheriff with some deputies went in pursuit of the mob. Unfortunately, the lynching had been done on a side road, and it took several hours before the body was found. The Sheriff and deputies saw the tire prints under a tree. The mob evidently had forced Shug to stand on the automobile with the rope around his neck. Then they tied it to the overhanging limb and drove the car out from under him. But the mob had vanished."

Norman told Ralph, "Now you see why I have these shot glasses." Then he swallowed another shot of whiskey without a chaser. He was tapping one finger down on the table consecutively. He explained why he had those shot glasses. It helps to limit his drinking during a time that was intolerable. Ralph understood and now his high was blown.

Norman signified that, "The mob hung him fifteen miles from Liberty and ten miles from Summit. "Right now, it has been four days to pass, and three Black Men have been hung on a tree on the side of the road, three days out of those four. Like this one, they all were taken from Blunder and the deputy sheriff at Summit, following his arrest on the charge of attempting to attack a white girl in the northeast part of Amite County." Norman explained to Ralph that while he was out and about town today how that scenario plays out. "Man, those white people were buying up some copies of the newspaper. The mob made a hit. There were reprints demand made and several hundreds of copies were printed so the patron and the public demand could be taken care of. Some Patrons bought a half dozen copies of the newspaper at a time for mailing to friends who lived far away." Norman wanted Ralph to know the powerful influence he had about his family as they always endeavored to take care of each other. "Anyone would love to be a part of you guys in every way. I'm not just talking. I know that you know this already. Your family sticks together, no one is going to hang anyone around you guys without a hell-of-a-fight."

All Ralph knew was his family just believed in being treated as a human being. "We will handle it right then and there. Harrison, that was some kind of story but what's most important, it's true. I have experienced more than enough, and I have seen plenty. Now my plan is, it's not happening to me. You got me here, now you got me drunk. What's next for a drunken man to do," Ralph stood up and said, "To take my drunk ass home." They all laughed, shook hands, and called it a night.

Chapter 6
Virgil Funeral Then a Miracle Happen

Sundays were always relaxing and about having fun most of the time. Thomas Pain's wife, Marilee Pain would take her son and visit her family in Brookhaven. Marilee was always excited when it came to visiting her sisters, Anne Marie Case and Marilyn Hardy. Jeremiah Pain was excited to be going to Brookhaven to visit his aunts and cousin.

As they were on their way, Jeremiah asked his mother, "Do you think Matthew would be excited to see me as I am to see him?"

Marilee replied, "Why of course he is, Matthew is always full of joy whenever we come. He never wants you to leave when it's time to go, he loves us, and loves playing with you. Don't ever feel that way, ok baby."

Jeremiah responded, "That's right mom, why wouldn't he be happy to see me, I love you mom."

As she rubbed his forehead, Marilee responded, "I love you too son, now that's my baby!"

As soon as they pulled into Marilyn's driveway the boys were off to playing. Marilee stopped Jeremiah and asked, "Where are your manners? Give your Aunt Marilyn a hug. Marilyn I'm going to use the phone right quick, I'll be right out," said Marilee.

"O.k.," Marilyn replied. "Jeremiah that's just what I needed, a huge hug," said Marilyn.

When Marilee finished on the phone, she joined her sister sitting on the porch in the rocking chairs while the boys were playing with some toys. "I'm so glad to see you Marilyn and I really need to ask you a question.

Marilyn answered in a soft voice, "I'm listening."

Marilee stated, "You know Jeremiah is so excited to be here, I don't want to interrupt them while they're having so much fun. Marilyn, is it alright to leave Jeremiah here until I come back from the cabin if you don't mind? I need to pick up a few important items, it won't take long."

Marilyn replied, "Marilee, of course you can, take your time."

She shouted, "O.K."

Marilee reached her destination and entered into the cabin. As soon as she entered, she went to the bedroom going right to the dresser drawer when these strong hands grabbed her hands and pushed her against the wall. Marilee whispered, "I saw your car outside Guy, you tried to hide it!"

Guy replied, "No talking." Clothes started dropping off

everywhere as they made it to the bed then she pushed him on it. Things got very intense when he lifted her up against the wall, hours later they departed and went their separate ways.

Thomas Pain had quite a few friends to stop by, all except Terry Hardy and Mark Child. The two men had other things to do but their friend, Teddy E. Smith was there. Their ages varied, with a few of them wearing straw hats, suspenders, and those conveniently wearing overalls that touched the soul that no man can go without. They sat around drinking tea while others were playing horseshoe.

The men were talking, pointing out how well the sheriff and deputy handled their jobs; and how the mobs saved people with their swiftness in handling the criminals' situation. One of the gentlemen took a sip of his ice-cold tea an indicated that, "After all, there were three niggers that were hung and they all were in one paper, the daily newspaper. Now, how can it get any better than that, you can believe this was the highlight moment.

Another friend described it to be, "The icing on the cake is what it was, and boys, it was sweet." The men laughed and played games while drinking their iced tea, enjoying every moment of that Sunday as a memorable one. This was news that everyone knew about, and everyone had their say about it. Let's just say that their remarks were more on the reserved side than unreserved.

Crops were steadily being planted and they were growing just the same. The Haynes stayed focused on what had to be done because every summer was hard, long, and hot. That was not what you would be looking forward to, working in the sun, doing summer. But they made the most of their time when they were working. Whether they were planting seeds, cleaning out the weeds, watering the crops or harvesting the crops, they made the most out of the situation. Singing was the peacemaker; it had expression, emotion, the depth of it all. The music was all around filling their internal souls for everyone who was right there stuck in that same situation. Even if you couldn't sing, you would have felt the impact. There was a bright light, brighter than the light that equaled a day and for that bright light lived in their hearts, which made up that light of their lives and this one would never dissipate. The children were always on their minds, and they were kept safe. In order to keep them safe they kept them close to their heart. Because what is safe when human beings are attacking human beings? Still, they stayed focused. The Haynes family knew what had to be done no matter what happened. So, Ralph was there with his family, keeping his eye to that light. He knew that anything could happen where he was living and knew that he would stand his ground. He wasn't afraid because he had his family there with him. There were innumerable things going on in his head right now and he didn't know what to do with it or how to fix it.

By the middle of the month, Ralph was sitting outside under a Weeping Willow Tree watching the children while they played hide and seek. Alma came out of the house. She had braids that hung down her back. It was like she's moving with the wind as she took each step. She was carrying Annie Bell, her baby girl, on her hip. She took a seat next to Ralph on the blanket then she leaned into him and kissed him on his lips. Mandy, the middle daughter, poked her head out from behind the tree where she was hiding and witnessed the kiss. So did Curtis, the son who was next to Mandy. Mandy started laughing before she could put her hand over her mouth. In the process, Mandy was discovered. Now Leo and Hazel left to be found. But for Mandy and Curtis, right at this moment, the sight of seeing their parents kissing; cause for a little more snickering. While Curtis looked for his other sister and brother, Mandy ran over to her parents and gave them both a kiss. They were surprised and happy about her reaction. Alma was smiling when she spoke to Mandy, "So you were the first to be found playing the game."

Alma started twirling Mandy's hair with her fingers. Something made Mandy laugh, and she threw her arms up, and said, "It was so funny." Mandy still didn't let them know about the kiss, which was what she was really laughing about. But she did let them know that the game hide and seek is one of her favorite games.

Ralph thought how fascinating the kids are engaged in a game he used to play when he was a kid. Mandy at age five, looked at him, bucked her eyes and the words rolled off her tongue, "No you didn't dad, that's funny." Mandy sounded very excited all at once, while looking dignified! Curtis found them and he jumped up and ran over to meet them. Baby Annie Bell, ten months of age, wanted to go with them to play too. She wanted to but they were too grown up for her to play with, for now.

Ralph looked at her and laughed, leaned closer to Annie Bell, and whispered, "Not yet, but your time will come soon enough little one." Alma leaned over and gently placed her head on Ralph's shoulder, with her arms around little Annie Bell.

Alma wanted Ralph to know how she felt with her sweet words. She let him know, "This is the most pleasant day for July, it's nice. The wind was blowing like there were angels waving their wings making the wind feel like feathers blowing upon you. You know God exists, and baby he doesn't play."

Ralph thought this was maybe his clue to say something and he intervened. "Honey what are you trying to say, tell me what's on your mind?"

Alma responded, "You know I love you, but I haven't told you why I love you. You know sometimes, you can see why one person loves the other. Either they look good to them or they're just fine. They could be good people with money, or they just want to be with somebody. Each one of the four is totally different."

Ralph reacted with questions, because now he felt he was placed in a category of just cause. Now he wanted to know, "Since you put it like that, which one do you think represents me?"

Alma noticed the attitude coming out of her husband which she hadn't expected. So right away she wanted to know if he was kidding her. Ralph made it very clear the answer was no, and better than that, "You know I kid you not, now, give me that kiss-, h-o-n-e-y."

Alma pointed out to Ralph that he's a good person and he's good with her—and the children----.

"I'm Ralph, sitting right here and you're saying I'm good with you, is what you're saying. Ah honey, now you mean I'm boring, I'm your husband, Ralph Haynes, I'm not boring."

"I will say this, and it will be crystal clear," as Alma spoke slowly, "Now you know how we love being together, how did the word boring get squeezed out of that? I say that because I love you every day unconditionally and remember this, there is nothing boring about us." Baby Annie Bell had fallen asleep, so Alma laid her on the blanket and laid her head on Ralph's lap. He played with her hair as Alma spoke, "Ralph you know your body is together, everything is right. She told him that he had that look as she looked straight up into his eyes and you're tall too." Alma didn't want him to get the wrong idea, so she gave him all of her attention in order for her to compliment the strength that he had in him. She wanted him to know that he was all of that and then some. She explained the reason she announced him being a good man, that's what got her attention. Alma told him that he was handsome, true enough and how she loves the way his face was shaped, narrow and small. "Those high cheekbones, small lips and your smooth mahogany skin that surround those huge dark eyes of yours. Damn honey, you have a head full of beautiful thick hair too." She thought about it and said, "Baby you have it going on." She told him not to mention that to her again because she might keep him there forever.

Ralph made a remark, "Well, I like this already."

Meanwhile, the kids were steady playing. Alma made another comment, "You're tall, slim and you're naturally muscular, what's not to like about that. You have the full package baby and that's what I love about you."

Ralph brought to her attention that there couldn't be a better timing that would mean as much as I love you saying it right now. "You know Alma, that's funny how we can sit here being so loving to each other and to our children, living under these situations. Some miracle way, we will manage through it all."

Alma made Ralph notice, "Now you see, that's what I meant, and you don't even realize that you're doing it. You're just a smooth brother, that's all." Ralph was chuckling as she spoke. Alma started speaking on how today feels like the weather that we have in the month of November. Before Ralph could say anything, Marilee called Ralph and Alma's name. Marilee came out on the porch to meet Ralph. She told him to answer the telephone. When Ralph came out of the house from using the telephone, he announced his father had died. He was in New Orleans when it happened. Everyone was in shock, then he walked off the porch and his family surrounded him. There wasn't a dry face in sight. They struggled with the children until everyone had calmed down, including themselves. Thomas Pain was speechless as he walked slowly into the house. Ralph told the family that the funeral was already arranged. A funeral will be held in New Orleans first and then the body will be transferred here for the funeral service on Sunday July 23, 1927. They gathered the children up and they rapidly proceeded into their house.

Unfortunately, the family was experiencing another sensitive situation that touched the heart deeply. Ralph lost his mother a year ago and she was his heart, but he knows he's not alone because Alma let him know that he's appreciated constantly. But this was different for Ralph. They were not someone he fell in love with later on in his life. They brought him into this world, through times that were good and bad, and they were always there, but now no more. Ralph feels like they are stepping into their parents' position. Now since both of his parents are deceased, this thought had never crossed his mind before, until now. Ralph felt like now he was experiencing a true-life adjustment. He also thought his parents had to have felt the same way at some point and time. He had that thought because he could vision himself moving into their position clearly now.

The children knew that they wouldn't be seeing their Grand Dad anymore. Alma did a great job of explaining to the older children what had happened. She explained how, "We all are here on this beautiful earth because God created us, and he made it possible for us to live here for a while. Something like a butterfly lives for a while, until it does what it's supposed to do and then it dies. Some of us have a longer time on earth to do things than others. But we go around from one place to another, in multiple colors, spreading our wings, until we reach a better place. That's where Grand Dad is right now."

Hazel responded with and ah. Alma looked at her other children and she could feel their sadness. "Grand Dad is watching us right now and he will be with us in our hearts," Hazel said.

"My love, your grand dad is in the most beautiful place in the world." They all managed to put a smile on their little faces. Alma wrapped her arms around all her kids as they wept.

"We love our Grand Dad so much," the children echoed. That moment gave Alma what she was seeking.

When Sunday came around, they had made plans for the children to stay with one of the relatives. That's how they always did things. They weren't big on taking children to funerals. Still there were plenty of relatives and the funeral was huge. People were there, they didn't even know. Ralph realized from other people how his father touched their lives. Ralph held Alma's hand tight while they were in the funeral home that was called, The Family Heart Funeral Home, in Pike County. After they made it to the burial ground, everyone seemed to be a little calmer, maybe getting some fresh air was helpful. Once the immediate family placed a flower on the casket, a family member by the name of A. A. Alexander approached Ralph. Alexander was glad to see Ralph again; it had been years since they had seen each other. Alexander reached over and gave Ralph and Alma a hug and said whatever you need, you don't have to worry. He asked Ralph what he's doing these days?

Ralph explained that his family was living on Thomas Pain's property as sharecroppers. Alexander didn't have any idea and he said to him in a puzzling voice, "Is that right, at Thomas Pain's place."

Ralph, who spoke in a strong voice, "That's right, me and my family have been living on Thomas Pain land for years now."

Alexander looked at Ralph and smiled and with the unexpected, he invited Ralph and his family to come to live on his land. He explained, "I'm always going, doing things you know, but my brother, you know Redd Bug, is there most of the time. I'll tell you what; I'll get back with you. Thomas Pain is in Summit if I'm not misstating."

Ralph quickly said yes. Alexander makes it clear that he'll find him, and he can expect to see him in a week. They shook hands on it before they departed. Conversations ran high and before long everyone was leaving the Funeral. Ralph and Alma made it home safe with the children. They were sad for a while, until Ralph decided to share something wonderful to everyone. Just hearing the news was hard to believe. They didn't want to focus on what had been discussed until they knew for sure.

"It sure does have a hell of a ring to it," Ralph told Alma as they laughed and then they started weeping, from a small light of hope to that dark place of grieving. If it weren't from reality, it would be a lot of fun. Days after the funeral, Ralph witnessed many of the same people who had attended the funeral. He wondered why some people seem so concerned for me, in the presence of a crowd. As soon as they see me again, they act as if they have never met me before.

As the days went by, they still had to work because the crops had to be harvested. They worked as hard as they always had. Every day they would sing and help each other to make it through the hard day's work. And would you know as the week ended, there stood A. A. Alexander. Ralph looked up and there he was, just as big as light but only bigger than light to Ralph on that particular Friday, at that particular moment. Nothing looked better than a man who keeps his word. Ralph didn't waste any time walking over to greet Alexander with a handshake that ended with a hug. Ralph explained that he was waiting to hear from him, first before mentioning anything to Pain. I had to be sure, explained Ralph.

Alexander was quite aware of what he meant. He stated, he made a wise choice. Ralph started walking with Alexander, across the land slowly while Alexander explained, "That they are ready to make the move now. We can do this now with no problem."

Ralph told Alexander that he needed to know that they owe Pain and before he could finish the sentence Alexander interrupted him to ask him how much he owed? Ralph didn't know the exact amount and that is what he needed to know. They walked right up to Thomas as they were talking.

Ralph introduced his cousin, "Mr. Pain this is my cousin Mr. Alexander. He came to move me and my family to his place."

Then Alexander spoke to Thomas Pain, telling him about having a home where his relatives can live. "I'm prepared to take them with me today. You can get the total amount Ralph owes you while we're moving everything and I will take care of that," Alexander assured him.

Thomas stated that it wouldn't take long to get that, and he wishes Ralph and his family the best of luck. The rest was too good to be true for Ralph but certainly it was final and real. Ralph was fortunate enough to have family members who cared about him at his worst. Paying a debt in this situation would be the beginning for more than a few black families. In order for a family to move from one farm to another, there was a debt that had to be taken care of. Every family was in debt. It didn't matter how much work a family contributed, that family still owed a debt.

Ralph and Alma didn't have any problems. They gathered their items and in the process of gathering them, they both were wearing that same look on their faces that expressed, there is a God and God really loves me. Alma and Ralph are so grateful.

Now they can express who they really are without the headache. Being   graceful and able, made them move rapidly as if they hadn't worked all day. Before the day was over, all of their merchandise was packed. Alexander paid their debt, and they said their good-byes to the Pain's Family, where they stayed long enough. They were on their way to a new place that would be called home and with people who were their family.

Archie Alphonso Alexander lived out from Summit, the ride wasn't a very long one, but Ralph wouldn't have mine if it did. They talked all the way, which took an hour before the driver reached their destination. They pulled up in the vehicle and a wagon to a large, white house surrounded with much land as far as Ralph could see. Everyone got out and Alexander pleasingly showed the family where they would be sleeping. Don't worry about your things Alexander stated, "It can wait until tomorrow."

Ralph, Alma, and the kids settled in quite well. The children wanted to look around to see what the rest of the house looked like before getting ready for bed.

Hazel was twelve years of age and she was the oldest of the children. Hazel yells, "We need to see the rest of the house. It may help in case one of us wakes up through the middle of the night and not know where we are. We will be so scared."

The other children yelled, "We'll be really scared."

Alma and Ralph both showed the children around the house since neither of them had seen this home before. They loved it with the high ceilings and there was even a piano that was in one of the rooms that the kids loved the most. Before they knew it, they were back at the children's bedroom. Alma was proud to say, "This room is where we tuck you in," and that's just what they did. The girls slept in one bed and the boys slept in another. An hour afterward, Ralph and Alma got a kick out of standing there for a minute watching their children sleep. They noticed how peaceful they were, just lying there. Ralph and Alma's main concern was their safety. They kissed each one of their children and politely whispered to them, to have sweet dreams.

Alma took Annie Bell with her to the bedroom while Ralph went and took a hot bath. Ralph had all kinds of emotions to hit him all at once, which left him with a sense of calmness. When he entered the bedroom, Annie Bell was sleeping in the bed next to them. Ralph could not wait to lay his body down. He was planning to give into relaxation completely. They were so tired when they awakened, they were the ones who didn't recognize where they were.

They thought it was the most beautiful morning ever when they awoke. Alma was staring out the window at the rain. She was happy watching the rain fall, which was amazing to Ralph as he watched her from the bed. That moment was definitely for Ralph to cherish because within the next three minutes the rest of the children were at the bedroom door. They cracked the door and peeked in the room, Hazel whispered, "They're awake."

The door sprung open, and all four children rushed in, full of energy saying, "Good morning!" The children gathered on the bed right next to their dad's. Leo, who was seven years of age, walked over to Alma to see what she was looking at, out of the window.

They both returned greetings, "Good morning children." Ralph asked, "Did everyone sleep like a bear, or did you sleep like a gorilla?"

One of the children responded, "Gorilla." Another one's response was a bear. Then there was another one, now a monkey. Everyone laughed and said, "A monkey!"

Leo replied, "Curtis, that's a good one."

The curtains were vibrating. There was so much energy in the room, as the children's little feet fickle back and forth. There was a sweet fragrance, the scent of flowers, blowing into the room from the window. Ralph felt so proud to have brought his family out of that type of bondage to safety. "It is what it is," Ralph said.

They all were getting ready for breakfast; A. A. Alexander was in the kitchen by the time Ralph and Alma made it to the kitchen. The children stayed in their room until breakfast was ready. Alexander showed them where the cookware was located. Alma started breakfast while Ralph and Alexander began to touch base. Alexander poured up three cups of coffee and each of them took a cup. Alma mentions how good the coffee tastes. Alexander explained how different coffee is. "After drinking many different types of coffee, you will eventually choose that particular taste that is outstanding, and just for you. You just know, that's the one you must have." Alma was pleased with the flavor of the coffee at hand.

"It's yummy and you did a very good job picking this one," said Alma.

Alexander points out that, "We must have something in common."

"Could it be that we're family?" Alma replied.

"Why thank you cousin, Alma," answered Alexander. Alma took her coffee with her as she moved around in the kitchen.

Alexander hoped the family was able to get to sleep alright. "Everything was fine, very comfortable and the kids, well what can I say, other than that, there were no complaints. You couldn't have stepped in there at a better time. Well actually you could have," as they all laughed. Ralph started telling Alexander how he never thought things would get any better. And how he just could not see beyond the state they were in. They just felt hopeless. Alexander knew exactly what he meant. Alexander was nodding his head in response to what Ralph was saying. Ralph said, "He thought about his children and how they, meaning black folks, end up dead and no one knows what happened. No one sees anything, or even hears anything, this is not living the full potential of a human being. We're not living in a civilized society."

Alexander agrees, "That it's hard, there is no doubt, but we have to stay focused on what we're trying to accomplish. We always need to be doing something to continue to rise. For instance, you and Alma made the decision that you both would stay together no matter what to survive and for the sake of your family. Man, that takes a special person, meaning a real heartfelt person, because that is where your time and energy goes. However, that doesn't stop things from happening around you. You are more determined than you think. God has to have something greater for us all."

On that note, they got up to help Alma with breakfast, but they took heed on the topic at hand. After breakfast was ready, Alma brought the children to the table to eat, and they all sat around the table for the first time in this home for the Haynes family. Alexander blessed the food as Alma kept Annie Bell close to her so she could make sure she ate her food.

Alma thought the topic that the men were conversing on was so interesting. She wanted to express how we all are here because of our ancestors who were brought here unwillingly. Then she put a spoon of food in Annie Bell's mouth. "They had to work, doing whatever they were told to do without a mumble. It was more like yes sir boss or yes ma'am and the nodding of the head. And our Ancestors were brought here for their personal satisfaction and with a price. Because of that price that they paid for our Ancestors, now the white's think this is too good to lose and should go on, and on, and on. But Abraham Lincoln was

President during the years of, 1861-65 and during his term he freed the Slaves, our Ancestors. We and I do mean we, have been shot down like an animal, hung from trees, drugged with body parts cut off, and beaten to death all of our lives living in the United States. But this is all we know, this is home for us, and will we ever be able to be left alone? Just from that kind of treatment, you know the kind that makes you feel that you are not human. You know, like one of God's children."

Ralph knew that black people have contributed abundantly under unfavorable conditions though the processes of living in the United States. And we wonder why we have to be so afraid for our family's life. But he will support and stand his ground before he lets anyone harm his family. There's a lot of pressure altogether but it's always said to be prejudice.

Ralph let A. A. Alexander knew his family was so thankful for him taking on such a huge responsibility on himself to show love for his family. They laughed and Ralph announced it to be known, that now his heart is smiling. Alexander told him that he would do it again without any hesitation. They finally stop talking long enough to finish their breakfast. They all shared precious time together in the kitchen while getting it organized; and they sat around talking a while longer. Afterward Ralph, Alma, and the children got familiar with the grounds of the house, and they got enjoyment out of doing something so simple. Alexander was about to leave when Alma insisted that Ralph should go with him. Alma and the children now would have their moments together and finish settling in.

Alexander was on his way to Brookhaven, he now had someone to talk back to. Alexander was always on the move, in his mind he thought when he wasn't going to attend to business, he would spend his time with people that he cared about. He had known these people all of his life. Alexander was twenty-seven years old and was loved by those who mattered to him. There were blacks who were doing exceptionally well and unfortunately there were those who were underprivileged. The same is true for the whites, only in their situation no one was found hanging from trees or made a symbol out of, for all to witness.

Alexander didn't dwell on what could happen because he was well aware of what could happen. But he wasn't afraid of any one or death as far as that mattered and Ralph was the same, which made it awesome. Alexander was on a mission. He was a student at Jackson State College and was out for the summer. But very soon school would be starting for the fall. Alexander would be finishing his senior year of college and receive his Bachelor of Arts degree in Science and Economics in 1928.

He saw the world as his oyster and that's how he went about his life. Some treated him with much respect and that played off so beautifully because he saw the good in everyone. Even when he knew exactly what this person was about, he still expressed hope, but he would let them know that he knew what was going on with them. His thing was, when a person had done wrong, he shouldn't just ignore the wrongdoing, as if it didn't happen. It should be exposed and displayed how it could have been dealt with, in a positive manner.

Alexander found himself in front of the West Side Meat Market, but it wasn't a coincidence. He would purchase his meats at the market because they were fresh and of good quality. When they walked inside, Alexander looked at Ralph saying, "Right here standing is not one but four of my friends, Guy Martin, Terry is the owner, Michael and Herbert Tucker, they are brothers, are we lucky or what."

Alexander stated, "Ralph Haynes is my relative." Guy looked at Alexander and tilted his head to the side because they hadn't seen one another for some time now. Guy wanted to know what Alexander was doing walking in on his territory. They walked toward each other until their hands united and they were smiling from cheek to cheek. Right behind Guy's hand shape was Michael's Herbert's and Terry's with a hand slapping together hand shape. All Guy Martin could say was, "What a coincidence and they say that coincidence doesn't happen."

Alexander started shaking his head, "Well, I'll be damn," he didn't have a clue Michael and Herbert were home again. He told them that he knew the government should be looking for the both of them because they were missing two good men. I know this was a surprise for the family. Alexander was elated. Michael was seeing whether it's safe to speak now but they reassured them that they love every moment. Michael told Alexander they came home at the first part of the year. Then they moved out of the way in case someone came into the meat market to make a purchase. Herbert expressed how glad they were to be home, and how they miss their wives and children. Being in that situation alone, Alexander knew the time away from your loved one would have to be stressful. Alexander wanted them to know that they admire badass men and shook hands again.

Alexander asked Guy, how was his wife? And in return Guy looked at Alexander then he replied, "Man don't ask me about my wife because you know she's fine." Guy and the brothers all laughed with Alexander. "You know when I get home and tell my wife that Alexander asks about her, she'll be looking for him to come visit, so be ready to eat, you know she loves to feed you for some reason."

Alexander was very happy to hear that, and he thanked God for that because he has witnessed that she can cook. Alexander made a speech, "I have learned, no matter how hungry you are, never sit down at anyone's table unless you know they can cook." Alexander decided to make his order while the other men were paying for theirs. He brought plenty of meat so everyone would be pleased. They talked until Alexander paid for his order. Then the men were ready to exit the meat market and Terry Hardy thanked them for their purchase. Then they all went their separate ways.

Chapter 7
A Better Understanding of Life

After a week had passed, the Haynes family was relaxed and adjusting well to their new environment. They had a chance to meet relatives and friends they never met before. It was a new beginning for them. Ralph and Alma were inspired to see families that were doing well for themselves. Ralph felt like a child in a candy store eating his first piece of candy. He was touched like never before because now he had something that he thought was unreachable. Hope is there, where there was none. He had love and it was strong, now he had discovered, by firsthand, the word hope.

Alma thought it was refreshing discussing with her family how they came about being related in the first place. Alma liked being able to explain, especially to the younger generation, to whom they're related. So, there would not be any bad feelings, or I am sorry I didn't know. There were open conversations, and everyone was honest and considerably pleased with what was happening. Alma thought, "This is more of a topic written as,

Not Ending up Marrying to One of Your Cousins." But for all it was worth, it sent sparks too many as they visited with family members. They were able to see who was their relative and who was not.

After everything that was happening, people had a need to feel that they were related to someone that they actually were not related to. Alma and Ralph had the chance to clear all of that misunderstanding. They were convinced there was something that person needed or maybe they wanted to feel close to a family who they admired and wanted to be a part of. We all want to be accepted and feel loved just being in the presence of someone. The feeling could be love or it could be showing respect to people who are in your presence.

There was one cousin that stood out in the crowd because of his light, brown, curly hair. His hair was pointing in every direction. There have been times when one may have thought that his hair had a mind of its own. Curly is what they called him, and he had a mind just as interesting as his hair. He mentioned the kind words from other people have left a lasting mark on the soul of our families. "But we won't go overboard about it," as Curly smiled and smiling was what he always did, especially when he said something that would ignite some brainstorming. That was one of Curly's specialties when talking to people. He would say whatever it took to reach and draw out something special within you, that you didn't even recognize it existed.

Ralph and Alma were actually comfortable with how

things unravel into something so beautiful. It has been a long and exciting day for everyone, and it was time to call it a day. It was late Sunday morning when Alma gradually opened her blue eyes to the sounds that were coming from outside. She eased out of the bed and swiftly moved toward the window. Alma sat on the floor with her arms resting on the window seal. She could hear from afar praying and singing. There weren't any homes anywhere near them. Still, Alma was captivated by this humming spiritual sound that filled the air, as if they were all at a gathering together. Alma's eyes were wondering until she finally spotted a group of women walking to church. As the women were passing through, Alma couldn't help but notice what they were wearing and how they were wearing it; and they were wearing it well. She was thinking how beautiful their dresses were. Their dresses were starched perfectly as they walked with dignity across Alexander's property. Every other detail that hung from under their dresses complimented the dress by adding to the flair of it. One dress had a nice bow that tied to the back and another with a bow that went around the neck.

All of the little things she thought made them look ever so graceful. All four of them looked like perfect dolls as they were passing across the grounds. She thought all four of them looked great, when we know at least one of them is supposed to be looking like a hot mess and end up getting everyone's attention. Because the other lady was dressed elegantly for their taste. Alma sat there letting her mind take over with thoughts.

Words spoken in a low tone by Ralph caused Alma to jump as if she was going to take off flying. Ralph started whispering to her asking her what she was thinking about? Alma grabbed Ralph pulling him over on the floor and asked him, "Why did you do that?" As they both laid there on the floor.

Ralph did what he did because it felt so damn good. He wanted to know did she feel damn good. Alma thought maybe he thinks I'm going to play this game with him. So, she responded, "Hell no!" She made it a point to let him know that he ran her blood pressure up to the max. They both laid there laughing at one another and stayed that way for as long as the children let them.

Later on, Ralph and Annie Bell were taking a nap while Alma and the rest of the children were outside. The children were playing in the yard while Alma was slowly passing by watching them. Then she noticed Frances Carter (A. A. Alexander's fiancée). Frances was just standing on the property looking over the land. Alma was walking over in her direction and Frances knew exactly who she was as she continued to approach her. Frances was excited to see her. She wanted to know if everything was working out.

Alma let her know it could not get any better than it is right now for her. But if it could, that could only mean that we would have our own place. Alma was in a great mood; she was better than she could ever imagine. She asked, "Frances can you see it? I know you can because it's going all through me, in and out." Alma laughed, telling Frances, "You know people say, God works in mysterious ways, and we have experienced it, many times firsthand. Knowing that, makes me feel really good from the inside out, through the process of not knowing when it will happen, you could almost worry yourself away to nothing."

Frances laughed with all of her might, as she wiped the tears from her eyes and raised her eyebrow. Then Frances added what she thought would contribute to what Alma was experiencing. She wanted Alma to know that sometimes it seems to take longer for something to happen when you want it or need it so bad. It's like saying, 'maybe I should have asked for it sooner.' Alma laughed and looked at Frances then she spoke in a deep voice, "Yeah right."

Frances spoke on what she noticed most of the time when she's praising the Lord while attending church. Today was no exception and she enjoyed the services, but sometimes she didn't stay focused, then she just looked up and asked God to forgive her. And today she was thinking, why there's not many men in church praising the Lord but there would always be plenty of women. Alma didn't believe her, asking if she was sure. Frances tilted her head as she turned to look at Alma because she wanted Alma to understand, she loves spending time in church, and she attended quite a lot. "I must tell you the men were not fruitful in that area."

Alma had to take up for the men, she knew men mean well and it really would be very cool for men to take a stand

and be very bold by getting involved or just attending. Nothing looks better than a man dressed in a suit. Then she spoke very softly, or a nice shirt and slacks. Better yet, that would work in men's favor, she said, "I would think. He could praise the Lord, and everyone could see how they look when they're looking their best because they would be at their best, Amen."

The children were in the background playing the game called, Patty-cake-baker-man, bake me a cake as fast as you can. Roll it, pat it, mark it with a B and put it in the oven for a baby and me. As they clap their hands to one another back and forward. There was laughter as they would tickle each other. Frances and Alma were steady having their debate. All Frances knows is women are known to be the family members who would be present in church with the children. And she knows it's a fact that women are in a greater position. "For one we are the ones that take the children to church. So that they can have their firsthand experience of going to church and attending Sunday School Classes."

Alma believed all men are in churches, they are on the pulpit, the choir, and they are our young handsome men that are in church every Sunday. She's not in church every Sunday but she does know there are men present. Maybe their presence isn't overflowing as we would like, but they are present. Frances was playing in the grass with her feet and believed, "Some people are called on to do God's work. Knowing this alone should play a major role in how you should live your own life. You know what I mean. She noticed that some in ministry forgets their roles. They begin to think that they are God and whatever they say is written in stone. There are those in ministry who are false teachers and the consequence from it all, is they have lost sight of something that is so precise which is their true purpose to love people and show them how to love back, praising the Lord. Because you can be a teacher without preaching but you cannot be a preacher without teaching."

Alma is cognizant of a world of men that has gone into the ministry as a career. "They should have the means it takes for people to comprehend the Lord's words, so everyone would be on the same page."

France admits, "It's always something happening that's crazy, the world is so messed up." She wonders what it will be like one hundred years from now. Alma laughed, thinking that sounded scary and asked Frances did she think she would be here with her?

Frances was happy and she yelled, "Oh yeah."

Alma called the children and they gathered under a tree. They taught them the song and they all started singing,

"He's got the whole world, in his hand

He's got the whole wide world in his hand.

He's got the whole world in his hand.

He's got the whole wide world in his hand."

They were rocking from side to side, hands were clapping, and they sang every verse. The kids really enjoyed themselves including Alma and Frances. The women planned to show the children a good time, so they ended up playing jump rope. Alma and Frances showed the kids their tricks for jumping rope. The kid's thought they were awesome; they couldn't believe adults could jump rope like they just displayed.

Alma and Frances knew the children were astonished with it all, there was no way they could not love it and they made sure of that. Now it was time for the adults to pull some string to reverse what they had started in order for the kids to jump rope and continue this merriment. Alma and Frances threw the rope and the kids started jumping like pros. Hours later, Alexander came out of the house and demanded everyone to come inside. Frances thought he's just jealous because they were having too much fun. When they entered the house, Frances' eyes got big as she took a deep breath intensely enjoying inhaling the smells of foods that she would soon be devouring. Alexander confessed that Ralph wouldn't let him have the credit all by himself. They admitted being guilty of out doing themselves.

Everyone washed their hands and met in the kitchen, and they all entered the kitchen together.

They all were seated, and Alma thanked the chef, because these guys can cook. "I can get used to this, I love surprises, and now the secret is definitely out. There was a lot going on right now." Alma kissed Ralph on his forehead telling him how unexpected and wonderful everything was considering he was supposed to be sleeping. Ralph couldn't say anything, he just smiled.

After everyone was seated at the table, Frances took the pleasure in saying grace. Afterward, Alexander was enjoying what was happening around him. He held his arms up yelling, "Let everyone enjoy!" The rest was simply the joys of eating. Besides, if you were there, you could hear that there was some serious eating going on there.

Alexander mentioned, "He was having a storage built out from the house."

Ralph replied, "That it looked like it could be almost finished with."

Alma told Toy (Alexander's nickname, Toy) that his "storage house was pretty darn huge, what are you going to put in there?"

"For a while now, I had in the back of my mind what is called my favorite things project," Alexander explained. "This would be a place to put all of my precious items and they would all be under one roof."

Frances stated, "I knew this was the playhouse that my sweetheart always wanted, and I was waiting for it to be completed." She thought he was the sweetheart and she wanted everyone else to agree.

Alma agreed saying, "Well you know that's how he is, a sweetheart, who knows what he wants to do."

Ralph even spoke up saying "I certainly understood probably how you women might see him, but Alexander made it clear, speaking on behalf of us, the men, it would be the opposite. Actually, you would love nothing more than saying something totally off the wall; but who wouldn't want to support him. Personally, I don't think Alexander could go wrong."

Alexander wanted everyone to notice that he was still sitting at the table. Then the adults held their glasses up and they all agreed, "With an Amen to that."

Alma excused herself from the table to take the children to their room. Baby Annie Bell had eaten herself to sleep, and Frances had no problem helping her with the kids. Frances loved telling the kids fairy tales. Hell, she tells them as if she had written them herself. As soon as they got the children ready for bedtime, Frances helped them to put themselves in that imaginary world through their mind. In the meantime, there was a knock at the door. As Alexander approached the door, to his surprise there stood Michael and Herbert Tucker. Alexander reached out at their hand and there also stood Terry and Guy. Now, Alexander was feeling like an invigorated man, this day has been a unique one. He didn't know if they had forgotten where he lived or what.

He welcomed them into his home and treated them like they were his brothers. Alexander mentioned the timing could not get any more convenient than this because they had just finished eating. The men couldn't believe that they had missed a great meal, as they looked at Alexander laughing. They wanted Alexander to know that he wasn't right at all. Then Ralph walked in saying, "I'm his favorite cousin Ralph, it's great seeing you guys again." The men respond, with handshakes. Ralph laughed as he shook their hands and they all gathered in the front room. Alexander started speaking on how he first met the two brothers and how they were always close and to know them, you know you had two great friends.

Herbert and Michael were speechless, but it lasted only for a second before they thanked Alexander. "Man, that's a really nice thing to say and your choice of words were excellent. I couldn't have said it better, myself," coming from the mouth of Michael and Herbert agreed.

Alexander wanted to know what's going on in Brookhaven and that he knew the families were doing well. Michael assured him they were living in the same neighborhood. Michael can't or he just didn't want to leave that area at the moment because it's more as a comfort zone to him with the feeling of being connected to something. Michael stated, "You know, it keeps me grounded and I will do whatever it takes to keep that balance, it's the good in my life."

Ralph was sitting across from Michael facing him, sitting there listening to him. He was staring him straight in his eyes and he let him know saying, "I could sense the experience you had endured, and it was a huge reality check for you both. The two of you did what you had to do; and you both came back home." Ralph gathered, just from hearing that, they were there for a reason. They make a difference and they're survivors out there kicking ass. Ralph said, "Don't get me wrong, I'm sure, all the other soldiers made a difference, whether they made a choice to go there or they were drafted. They say God won't put anything on you that you can't handle, with that said, we're glad you're home."

Michael's feelings skyrocketed when he heard Ralph's words. It's what his mind needed to hear. The mind is a powerful thing and when it's working along with the use of words, it's an almighty combination working together, and all Michael could say was, "Thank you Ralph." Ralph nods his head and smiles.

Alexander excused himself from everyone and returned with glasses on a tray and their favorite drink, which was Brandy to help moisten their throat as they spoke what they knew were true.

Herbert knows things happen. He said, "It's like you try to do what you can in this world. You want to make a difference, but you really have to be strong because unforeseen shit be going on. There are things that's wide open to us that go on." People can be extremely cursed and he's not only talking about whites but blacks as well. "It's hard talking about one race doing wrong to another race, when the race that's being treated wrong is nasty to their own race. So sometimes it gets hard trying to live a decent life when there's much chaos going on. People need to live their life as normal as possible in order to begin living that part of their life that is meant for them." He wanted to know if he had said it right. Everyone let him know that he was accurate.

Terry said, "It sure is nice hearing someone tell something, deserved to be heard. You need to know how much both of you are appreciated."

Ralph's response was "Yep, he said a mouthful then, you are actually faced with intimidation from both sides. That makes it twice as hard for blacks and in that particular situation it feels like everyone is focused on you and there is no way out. It would be hard to concentrate and stay in that right state of mind when people are being the most iniquity. How can you have a life trying to live being surrounded by that kind of illness?"

Michael let Ralph know, "You have a point there. I honestly believe a person like that can't have happiness in their life. They would have to be extremely unhappy, just darn right out miserable. Acting like they have it going on, and - that's – all – that – is… acting,

What Ralph understood from all of it is people feel empowered when they can control a person. In order to get the respect that they never had, and they always wanted to be looked up too. Now they can play it out to comfort that feeling they always had. Then Alexander arrived with the refreshments and explained to the men that, "The women were making their rounds and when they made it to the kitchen, unfortunately, he was leaving. So right now, they are still busy doing what women do."

Speaking about leaving, Ralph asked, "Toy (Alexander) how soon are you heading back to school, and are you ready?"

Alexander was impressed that Ralph showed interest in him going to school. He informed him that school would be starting sooner than he expected but the answer is in about a month. He felt like he had been attending school forever. He had spoken about a vision of pushing himself hard to do what he had to do. He stated, "My plans are to work with the young people to push them hard as well. We need our young people to be as keen as possible in the mind. I'm convinced they will eventually come face to face with the pros and cons of their decisions and all of the pure evils that are out there. They should be able to identify the difference in order to know the safest destination to take."

Guy shouted, "Yeah, it is bad when you're in a situation, where you can't see any way out. There might be someone who is passionate enough to not just understand or talk about it because you know we can talk about people, until they are six feet under and never left a hand to actually do something about it. It might take this, to educate people so they can grow to be copacetic about themselves and can help to make a difference in this crazy world before we stomp them six feet in the ground."

While Terry directed his attention to Alexander, he was expressing that there are many level headed young people and old alike and they're not doing what they could do with what they got. "They either don't know what they're capable of achieving, maybe it's because their environment has engulfed them. Or they just don't care. Toy, you are a good, good man from a great family with everything it takes to live a great life." They all held up their glass as Terry continued, "We all know that you will conquer, and you will make a damn difference, or you will die trying brother." They all shouted Cheers, as they took a sip of their drinks, smiling proudly.

Michael remembered when they were in their early teens. How they had never played hooky from school before. So, his brother and Alexander had decided to meet where there were not any people around. Ralph laughed, knowing that was a big moment that they could get in trouble and that could be bad. "Real bad for the home boys," Ralph stated.

Michael continued telling how they started out just walking around because they didn't have any knowledge where they were going. "Then Herbert came up with an idea. We would walk to a store that wasn't far away and purchase candy, sodas, and some cookies to take with them. There was a huge red barn in an open field that took about thirty minutes to reach from the store, but we had never actually been there. When we reached the barn, man, that barn was the best. There was hay all in the front and on the side of the barn with a window that was opened on the top in the front of the barn. When we entered there was a ladder that reached all the way up to the window. Man! That's when the fun began. We put the snacks down and started up the latter. Alexander was first to jump down, and it felt like we were flying then we hit this huge stack of hay."

Then the three men said together, "We rolled down those stacks of hay!" They all laughed out loud.

Michael continued, "Man that was it. It was about two weeks later, there were men working around the barn area. There was a pond farther out from the barn. One of the men that were working, raked up a water moccasin, not knowing of course, stroked the six-foot-long snake with a pitchfork and that's when all hell broke loose. The moccasin got in a position to strike. The man with the pitchfork started striking at the snake, then it did an about face and started chasing him. Venom was spraying from the snake's mouth as it chased him. The other worker grabbed a hoe and started chopping up the snake. Those men still talk about their witnessing the water moccasin that curled into that striking position and how amazingly huge it was with prints on its skin that was so beautiful, and how the prints alone would have you in a trance without you even acknowledging it. Before it was completely over, the man who had the hoe, leg was burning from small portions of the venom that had splashed on him while they were in the process of killing the snake."

Wow, said Terry and Ralph, they were flabbergasted. Guy said, "That's some kind of story. You guys are lucky to be alive to tell this story."

Alexander was sure they were fortunate upon remember what happened. "Yes, and that was the first and the… last of playing hooky from school."

After Herbert heard the story and played it over in his head said, "Playing hooky didn't feel meaningful after that. We went to school with pride and feeling great about being there. Yeah," Herbert stated, "we were fortunate then, and like tonight being blessed with this good food just for being here."

Michael remembered a situation that could have been one of them as well. "It happened a couple of weeks ago. Yeah, we could have ended up like Mr. Benson, you never know. Oh, except for you Terry, no offense."

Terry replied, "None taken. You know Mr. Blake Benson, didn't you Toy?"

Alexander answered, "I don't know him."

Terry said, "He was always walking; he was a very friendly person, that's all I knew about him."

Alexander wanted to know if he was injured badly, because he had heard about the unfortunate incident. Michael made it very clear that, "Mr. Benson wasn't injured badly, not at all. Benson was killed on the spot."

"Yeah," Guy replied, "I had heard."

Terry said, "The same here."

Ralph wanted to know if he was drunk because he could have been drinking and was the reason for him getting hit by a car.

Michael stated, "He knew that the situation was an unfortunate one. Blake Benson didn't drink. If he had been drinking, maybe he would have fallen off the road before he was hit. It happened around 6:00 p.m. on a Saturday, and this wasn't any different from the others. Whereas no one saw anything. Men, he was walking the street, speaking, and stopping to talk to friends along the way. Then he was ran over by a hit and run driver."

"However," Herbert stated, "I knew that everyone who had the pleasure to be greeted by him was tough. After his wife reached him, she put her arms around him and held him. It was nothing nice to see. Friends started comforting her as she gradually released him. He was then taken away and the crying sounds that echoed in the street soon vanished as the crowd slowly dissipated."

Ralph replied, "One thing I know about death is I've seen more than my share of it for now. We don't know when we're going to leave here. Death is never easy but this way - this way is never the way anyone should have to go. Their loved ones will have this in their memory forever. I didn't know them but hearing this story, my heart goes out to his loved one."

Guy emphasized, "We all need to be aware of everything we do so we don't become a victim. Terry, this does not have anything to do with him."

They all laughed as Terry said, "You never know." He reminded everyone, "This has been a night to remember for all of us. We blessed the food, now it's time for us to bless ourselves up and out of here."

Alexander laughed telling Terry, "You know man you always had a way with words." After they shook hands good-bye, they wanted to stay grounded.

Chapter 8
Telling It Like It Is

This is the beginning of the month of August 1928. The following day was an early one and Alexander had something to announce to Ralph and Alma. He didn't quite know how they would react. As they sat on the back porch, the scenery for breakfast was the deep greenery of the trees. Trees that had vines that entwined about the limbs with a bundle of small beautiful blue blooms that hung down from them. So relaxing, the perfect scenery as Alexander spoke the words, "Are you ready to move into your own home?"

Alma turned her head so quickly toward Alexander, he got scared. She was wondering, "Did he say what I thought he said?" Then she whispers, "What did you say, did I hear you say, your own home?"

Alexander spoke loud and clear, "That's what I said."

Alma leaned closer to Ralph as they looked eye to eye at each other and they both started screaming as they embraced.

They finally manage to stop screaming. Alma was shaking and mumbling and then words flowed from her mouth saying to Ralph, "Oh honey we did hear that, it's true, but I can't believe it. That sounds like heavenly music to me." Then Alma moved swiftly towards Alexander to give him a hug tight enough to kill a bear. Ralph shook his hand and from that to a hug.

"Ralph, baby how long have you known about all of this," asked Alma?"

"Alma honey, Toy probably knew I couldn't keep a secret as massive as this. I am only a man and there's only so much I can handle at once. Baby, this is my first, and it sounds better than anything I have heard in a long time. We didn't believe that we could be made any happier than we are right now, I mean before this happened. You, Alexander, have made us extremely happy again. How can we begin to repay you?"

Alexander answered. "Just keep loving and taking care of your family as you have been doing. Being there for your family is all you need to do for me. That will bring the highest light and the beauty of your life."

Frances was sitting there taking advantage of the warm feeling that was being embraced, which brought tears to her eyes. She thought she had seen everything that was possible to see about her soon to be husband. Right then at that moment she knew she would be spending the rest of her life with this man. But the greatest of it all, she knew that she was in love with him, and their love was going to last forever.

Everyone took their time eating breakfast, for the children had eaten earlier. When they finished eating, everyone walked to the place that Alma and Ralph had been curious about. Of course, that was Alexander's storage house. Walking to get there was like taking a little stroll to get there but they felt like they were floating and there they were in front of their lovely home. Alma couldn't believe the word he said. She kept repeating it, plus saying can you believe this. It had a fine sound to it as she opened the door and they all entered. They could smell nothing but the aroma of fresh wood, all through the house, brand new and cute as a button.

Frances was happy for them, she can see them now enjoying their privacy, "All of you are going to love it here. Alexander will have it furnished so don't worry about that. Then you can move when it's completed and that shouldn't take too much longer, right honey." Alexander agrees that everything will be to their liking.

The rest of the children entered their new home. Leo was ten years old. He was next to Hazel who was the oldest. Leo was curious and started asking his father, "Is this where we're going to live, dad?"

Ralph squatted down and put his arms around him with a squeezing hug and said, "Yes, we are. We will have many wonderful times here."

Leo then gives him a tight squeeze with tears flowing down his face as he murmured, "Oh dad I can hardly wait."

It would be just a few weeks before the Haynes family moved into a house that was paid for. It was a gift and not just a house but a home that they own. Now the family had a new life and a new beginning on this blessed land. By the time the Haynes moved into their home, Alexander was off to college at Jackson State, doing what he loved best. One of the things that he loved about Jackson State was its history. He didn't just attend Jackson State he sought this college's history, and this is what he found.

Jackson State College was established in 1877 in Natchez Mississippi. It was operating as Natchez Seminary, which was a private school. The Natchez Seminary was under the auspices of the American Baptist Home Society of New York. And its purpose was to educate the newly freed slaves between Memphis and the Gulf Coast of Mississippi.

The Natchez Seminary was serving as an Educational Institution that primarily trains Ministers and Teachers, the school enrolled twenty students at that time. The school also owned a single piece of property and the building that stood on it was a converted Civil War Marine Hospital.

Serving as the first president was Dr. Charles Ayers. The school prospered in Natchez until November 1882 when American Baptist Home Society moved it to Jackson, a more central location in the state. Because of this knowledge, A. A. Alexander was proud and honored to attend a school with such a remarkable history.

For Alexander learning new words, reading, and educating himself. This made him stronger, especially when it came to learning more Black History. Whenever he needed a pick –me-up, he could always read a piece of information about people of his own race. One thing he did know was, there's no reason for a Black Person to not overcome their bad situations that they are in. We can help each other, at least the ones that want to be helped.

Rev. T. S. Newman, who lived in Dallas Texas, was one of Jackson State's biggest fans. He's a long time, standing friend of Alexander. He is the Founder of Goodwill Radio Hour and Goodwill Youth Council of the Southland, Inc., Rev. Newman would send Alexander some editorial notes that he thought would be interesting and useful.

Rev. Newman sent Alexander his own expression of opinion of himself. He also included a bonus that Alexander would find to be rewarding as his listener had. Rev. T.S. Newman wrote, "First of all, I was born in the south, worked in the south, and received what education I have as a Negro, was in the South. I have worked with White Brothers from the farmlands to the back alleys of city streets. I feel I can talk about the face problem more than anyone in the Northern Parts of the country. Personally, I feel like most Negroes feel that they live in the South. We have learned to live and work with each other with a peace of mind and each holding his distinctive place in life. We have sore spots. Yes, the white and the black man can recognize the sore spots that's brought about by ignorance on the part of both sides. They have brought pain to both, but much has changed in the south, blacks have improved their salary, schools, churches, and recreational facilities are better." You could feel the intensity when he said, "We are talking about correcting past mistakes."

"In the South, the blacks can call upon their white friends when things get rough. There has always been some love and help there. That is the difference between the Southern Negro from the Black race, but they are no different than any other race. There are many things you may have noticed that the blacks are not seeking as a solution for our problems. There haven't been any problems seeking force, communism, and agitation of radicalism. Those who are in their right mind know that time, religion, cooperation, training, education, and tempered with Good Will, will bring about the solution of our problems.

He wanted what he was saying to be clear: "That Blacks need to realize this for themselves I can't blame them for this. You probably can think of thousands of reasons for the sit back. There is still much to be accomplished, there is no need to make him feel the height has been reached or can be reached quickly, when he just recently started. Certainly, when compared to the White Americans, his time has been cut short. Don't be misled by many agitators who want you to believe that you have caught up with the ones that are several hundred years ahead of you. Whatever happens, with time it will be an honorable race. Let your mind wander back a hundred years to see where Blacks were, then compare it with now and see the race has come a long way. It is by many that Atlanta Georgia is the central point of education, finance, culture, and business. There is no other place that can be called the Negro Capital of the World. You can't name any other place where the Blacks control and own with much power than in the South.

"Keep pulling off the scab to make fresh wounds, is an expression used to describe the agitators and the so-called Liberators. To my mind, these efforts are designed to do away with the whole pattern of segregation and to establish an integrated social order in which there will be no distinction in this country, on the basis of race, religion, color, or nationality. I feel this is not the solution to the race problem. God made a distinction between races, so why should mere man try to change it? There would be no rejoicing in reading the book of history to find that Negroes had lost this racial identity and the racial heritage. I'm concerned for the Blacks because if this comes about in the long run the Blacks will be set back another fifty (50) years. By paying attention, I found that a Negro that's in the Northern States can attend most of the schools without any problem. Most of the Northern States who educate him will not hire him as a teacher.

"Let's say the state of Connecticut, for instance, it doesn't have twenty-five Negro teachers. As far as I'm concerned, I would take my direction toward the South. Not anywhere near proportionate representation. Every device you can think of, was used in order that the Negro would not be assigned to a teacher job, to be qualified for, then was turned down. A reputable New York Labor Union made a survey on the Employment of Negro Teachers. The survey explored a systematic plot that was signed to exclude Negroes as teachers.

"My dear reader," he stated, "I only call them as I see them as an ace an ace, and a spade a spade. My people, the Negroes, have millions of dollars that goes into their hands, throughout the south. With the Good Will and the help from our white friends, in time we will create our own standard of distinction, it will be so effective that others will seek it. I'll say it again with time, training, education, and living what we preach with more real Christianity."

How refreshing, A. A. Alexander thought. He felt as if he had been made over, it gave him a sense of power. This reverend knew the direction Alexander was headed and this information was the key. Now Alexander knew he would be able to put most of his attention where it would be the most accountable. He would be able to see the difference from his effort that he's planning on accomplishing. But right now, his friend Rev. T. S. Newman was the one he was proud of. Alexander would make sure to go home every chance he got, and right now was a good time. As soon as Alexander reached his hometown, he was eager to see Frances. She lived with her parents, the Carter's in Summit. They were attending the same school when they became close friends.

As time passed, they grew closer and became inseparable. She was important to him because she complemented his world, which made his life complete. When the two of them were together, the time that they shared was well worth it. Alexander didn't stay long; he just wanted to see Frances and spend time with her and her parents. Afterwards he headed home to see how Ralph and the family were adjusting. When he arrived, he walked over where Ralph lived. Ralph answered the door and to his surprise, there stood Alexander.

Ralph immediately welcomed his cousin home, as they bump their fist together. They took a seat and Ralph told Alexander that Mandy, their five-year-old daughter, "was so sick, she was just lying there lifeless. Frances had heard about Mandy, and she came to her rescue like an angel. She's been helping Alma with Mandy and the rest of the kids."

Alexander thought that was weird considering he just left her, and she didn't mention what had happened. "So, what is wrong with Mandy, did you find out?"

Ralph had to admit, they don't know. "Mandy was so weak that we were afraid that we would lose her. As the minutes dragged on my heart felt like it was beating, doubling its time. Tuesday morning, Mandy was given a medical examination by Dr. Lark. When Dr Lark finished checking her, he scratched his head and said, 'I'm sorry but I could not find anything wrong with her.' Alma started stroking her hair. Her hair hung all the way down her back. Her braids were as thick as your arm. Dr.

Lark said, wait a minute. He pointed his finger at Mandy's hair, 'that's it -- that's it!' Alma shouted, 'What is it?' Dr. Lark's medical diagnosis was that her hair is the problem. I'm sure you will see the difference in your daughter's health if I cut her hair off, over half of her hair in length at least. Dr. Lark got a pair of scissors and asked, do you want me to do the honor or will you? I gave Dr. Lark the go ahead because they couldn't carry it through. Dr. Lark proceeded to cut her hair, right then and there.

"Dr. Lark's scissors and the thickness of Mandy's hair gave him a good workout for his money. When he finished cutting little Mandy's hair, Dr. Lark cleaned his scissors off and put them away. He was ready to call it a day. This is the Doctor's order, if she gets any worse don't hesitate to give me a call. Then he gave Alma a pat on her back, she'll be alright then he left. Just as one day ended another began, that's how fast her strength returned. It was amazing how her small fragile lifeless body came back to life after a bad case of the hair that grew too thick and too long, that almost drove them crazy."

Alexander was amazed at the outcome. He never thought Ralph would be saying something as simple as that. Alexander stated, "I was thinking something terrible was wrong. I'm not saying that wasn't life threatening within itself. This is my first time ever hearing something like that happening but there's always a first time."

Ralph stated, "All I could think of was the first time of our acknowledgement of her sickness and then watching her condition worsen. There were high and low periods of her being helpless. Then there were us, not being able to help her. Who would have guessed that your own hair could stoke your growth!" Ralph yelled, "A doctor, I guess! She was about to lose her life because of this condition. It seems unnatural for something like that to happen."

Alexander looked up and to his surprise, Mandy walked right up to him smiling and gave him and Ralph a surprising hug. Ralph had to have a moment to breathe when Mandy walked in the room. They were shocked by her recovery and being able to walk into the room. Alexander was touched, children have a way of making you feel special and loved and they don't even realize it. It just comes natural for them. Alexander placed her on his lap and just smiled. She was weak and moving slowly but best of all she was moving. Alexander was treating Mandy like the princess she was. Ralph gave her a kiss and whispered in her ear if she felt alright?

Mandy replied, "I feel great. I miss you."

Alexander answered, "Oh yeah, do you think a ride will make you feel greater?"

Mandy bucked her eyes and said, "It might, oh can I, daddy?"

Ralph answered, "Let's tell mom first!"

Alma walked into the room and said, "I heard you honey. Oh, my baby is awake. Did she walk in here?"

Ralph answered, "Yes she did honey, and we were really

astonished."

Alma gave Mandy a hug saying how much she loves her as she was stroking her hair with her hand.

"Please Alma, Mandy is going to love the journey ride," said Alexander.

Alma stated, "The ride should help uplift her, I would think. Ok, I know she will enjoy the ride with you. Right now, I'm going to take a nap with the other kids, these aching bones can use it." Alma gave Mandy a kiss and they went on happily and so did Alma.

Alexander decided to add a little twist in the journey. Ralph was really focusing on Mandy. The expression of happiness was smeared all over his face. The thought of losing another member of the family brought the family to a reality closeness. Alexander mostly listened to the two of them. Watching them put him in touch with their feelings and that feeling was deeply felt. He drove up in front of the South Side Meat Market. He told Ralph that he would be right back. Before long, Terry Hardy walked out with Alexander. Alexander was carrying several packs of meat under his arm as they chatted before he came back to the car.

They were on their way back home and the journey would soon come to a delightful end. Mandy made up for the time when she was sick and too weak to speak. She was able to fill that need very quickly. After they reached the home front, the rest of the family was glad to see Mandy in such good spirits with that bright smile they all loved. Although she missed her hair, her parents let her know that hair will always grow back and then some. Alexander was pleased to be able to help out. Now he can spend even more precious time with the one he desired the most and that would be Frances, his fabulous fiancée. That weekend was filled with passionate caring that was nourishing to the soul.

Saturday morning, there were strange sounds that weren't the sounds they normally heard around here. Ralph got up to see what it was, and Alma was right behind him. The first person they saw when he opened the door was Alexander. Alexander knew what the problem was when the door opened. Actually, he was expecting that reaction and he responded accordingly. "It's 6:15 in the morning and it's a Saturday morning. It's too noisy to sleep." Alexander admitted it was his fault stating, "I admit, I'm guilty."

Alma and Ralph spoke at the same time wanting to know what was going on?

Alexander laughed, suggesting that they should walk with him. They walked behind their house and from a distance they could see cattle. They knew there weren't any cattle yesterday. Alma looked at Alexander with a smile on her face expressing how fine the cattle looked. Alexander informed the both of them that, "The fence is the reason they were disturbed so early this morning. They were making sure the fence was secured. You know I will be back and forth for a while, so I don't have any reason for cattle." Alma made a squealing sound, just when Alexander announced, "The cattle is yours, for the keeping."

Ralph and Alma embraced after hearing such marvelous news. Alma was confident she was going to need some breathing therapy lessons, so she won't forget how to breathe. She didn't know how much longer she could handle this wonderful news that kept advancing, at such a rapid pace. Ralph looked at Alexander with a calm face, then the calmness transformed into a smile and from that smile to a thank you. For starters, Ralph wanted Alexander to know he could handle the unexpected, especially when it is this considerably.

Ralph knew about certain cattle and this one he knew was called Jersey cattle. He knew enough about cattle, to not have to worry about it taking up much of their freedom. Which means, there will be more time to share with his family? "We are looking at six nice Jersey dairy cattle," as he began to laugh, the laugher got louder.

Alma didn't know what to say to Alexander, and just the thought of her not saying anything was scary for Ralph. He couldn't believe she was speechless. Alexander couldn't believe it either as he leaned toward her and gave her a hug and just held her saying how happy he is for them to stroll into his life. Tears were flowing down her face as she managed to say, "How amazing. You have gone out of your way to show us how much you appreciated us, and you accomplished that." He released her and she threw up her shoulders staring at Alexander saying in a heartfelt voice, "We can't thank you enough for this? Our families or anyone, as for that matter, has ever done anything for us that would touch what you have done in such a short time. This is God's will, and He will bless you for this."

Alexander thanked her for the kind words, but he reminded both of them that it's alright to wear your heart on your sleeve. He knows they have a heart, and he knows they are human, most of all, he didn't want them to worry about anything because he already knew how they felt. Alexander just did what he felt was needed. He knows his family was blessed for a reason. They worked hard like everyone else, and they were paid. They spend their money with common sense or what they thought was common. His parents have always helped to improve others who deserved to be helped. He wants to do the same as his parents because it worked great for them. He knew they always stayed grounded.

This is a wonderful day and Ralph was ready to indulge, in something that's mouthwatering and would make them happy. He didn't know what that sounded like to these guys, but it sounds like getting a bite to eat for him. Well Alexander assured them, there wasn't anything for them to do because the men will finish everything. He informed them, that's what he was talking to Terry Hardy about at the meat market yesterday. It took a minute for Ralph to respond. He had to stay realistic and keep up with what's happening now with what Alexander just spoke on. "Oh yeah," said Ralph. "I remember what was said when we took Mandy for a ride." They laughed and got ready for breakfast. They all stayed close to home, after all the men were still working on the fence.

Early Sunday morning September 4, 1927, Alexander was restless. He left after he got dressed and headed out on the road. Alexander had contacted Michael and Herbert Tucker. The brothers contacted Guy Martin, and he agreed to be there. They were going to meet at a place where they could talk and just enjoy themselves in a different environment, somewhere out from Brookhaven near where the Tucker brothers lived. The people that owned the place knew them. The sat down and Alexander had a soda but the brothers like the foam stuff better. The brothers had the respect they deserved because of the way they carried themselves. They represented goodness and made others feel proud as they were captivated being in their presence.

The men were well settled in after reaching their destination. They were enjoying the moment when Guy Martin walked in. With his presents their tribe was completed. Guy was so excited to see his gang. All Guy wanted to know was, "What in the hell Alexander was doing, drinking a soda with all of this real alcohol in the air.

They all told Guy to come over here and take a seat. "You know nothing can really happen without you anyway." Well Guy agrees they could not celebrate one thing without him being present. Then he noticed there were ladies across the room that were definitely paying attention to them, and he brought it to their attention.

Michael reminded him that it's always nice having attractive scenery. While Guy was putting in his order at the bar, he told the bartender whatever those young ladies were drinking, put the amount on his order and have it sent to them. Then Guy joined the gang, and they were having a good time. Each of them enjoyed telling their stories, which were few true and many lies. But they all were well received and appreciated. After all was said and done Alexander spent the rest of the day with his family and Frances before he went back to Jackson State.

While sitting in the living room, Ralph and Alma started focusing on using what they already had to help enrich their life. They had plenty of time to prepare for what they were going to use in doing what they knew best and that was farming. Meanwhile Mandy was in the back yard near the cattle when she saw this old white man driving up. As he drove closer toward Mandy, she didn't move an inch or blank an eye. When he stopped, he offered Mandy four vehicle tires for one of those young heifers. Mandy didn't see the tires but from her gut instinct she knew what to say and her answer was no sir, the heifers are not for sale. He still tried but he was not successful, Mandy stood her ground.

As he drove off, Mandy remembered that her daddy used to do some work for him from time to time. Ralph saw Charles Harbor driving off from Mandy and went to ask what was going on. Mandy told him immediately what had transpired. Ralph let her know, "If something happened like that again to make sure to let your mother and I know. But my little girl is growing up being smart and beautiful. Come on Mandy, your mom is waiting for us.

Ralph and Alma had already been discussing what would be the best alternative for the cattle. Ralph left early that next morning. He knew what it would take to walk with a young heifer from where they lived to town. Ralph was well equipped. He would not be caught without his .38 revolver in his right-side pocket. He felt there could come a time when you only have one chance to save your life and he wanted to be able to have a fair chance of saving himself and his family's life. So, he always kept her close.

Ralph had to walk a couple of miles to take their young heifer to the auction. That heifer was the only company he had to talk to along the way and he used that time well. Ralph arrived and was amazed to see all of the people there. Ralph walked up on Mark Child and Thomas Pain, which meant something great happening for him. He was excited and by now he had already formed a picture in his mind of the outcome. He got his young heifer tagged and it was ready for the showing. Ralph watched quietly, as there was much to see, and it all had his attention involved.

After a couple of hours those who had merchandise to be auctioned off were pleased with their outcome and Ralph was no exception. Heading home always felt good but today walking with extra money in his left pocket certainly helped balance out the weight of the gun in his right pocket. Ralph walked straight and tall, long legs and all. It just didn't seem like a long walk as he headed home feeling unusually energetic.

Entering his home, he found Alma reading to the children. All of a sudden, they saw dollar bills flowing down around them. Ralph yelled, "Daddy's home."

The children had the most fun playing with the money as they were happily picking up dollar bills.

Alma was proud of her husband as she was hugging him thinking how he successfully attained it. The two of them joined their children in their playful moments. Those playful moments evoked memories of Ralph's childhood.

Alma tilted her head looking at Ralph as she noticed how tired he looked. Ralph repeated how nice it was to be at home as he went to take a bath. He went into the bedroom to change his clothes, but He laid on the bed for a minute, before getting up. Unfortunately, to his surprise he couldn't get up. He felt as if something or someone was holding him down. But for sure, he didn't see a soul. He came to a point where he could move and that's when he got up. Ralph started walking toward the first door and a young woman started talking to him. But he didn't comprehend what she was saying. Then she left out the door. He just felt very tired and went back to bed. As soon as he got back in the bed, he was totally relaxed.

Then it started all over again, not being able to move, like he was being held down again. He had struggled to the right side of the bed. Ralph didn't know what to do, so he yelled, "Jesus, Jesus," he still couldn't get up. Then he cried out loud saying Jesus Christ, and again Jesus Christ. Right before his eyes something started lifting up at the foot of the bed over on the left side of the bed. As it rose higher, the bed cover was lifting up with it and he could see what it was shaped like. It was shaped like some creature by the length of his arm. He wasn't sure if he really wanted to see what it looked like.

First Ralph closed his eyes and started speaking in a serious voice, repeating, "I rebuke you in the name of Jesus Christ." Ralph opened his eyes and it had disappeared, and to his surprise, he found himself in a cold sweat. He thought, "What was that? He said to himself, "I was dreaming! Oh LORD, I hope I was!" Ralph cried.

Ralph got out of the bed, sat on the edge of it, and looked straight up at the ceiling thanking God that it was only a dream. "What a hell of a dream that was." Ralph tried to shake it off as he got ready to relax in a tub of warm water. To Ralph, this warm bath water was the shit and that's all that mattered to him right then. As he was bathing, his thoughts were on his father and how he missed him. He laughed when he thought about how his dad ran into the woods after he had whipped Thomas Pain with his belt. "I'm able to laugh now about something that wasn't laughable during most of those examples of trials and tribulations. Now when I think about the things he did, I laugh because if I told people about this, they would have doubted it." As Ralph was finishing his bath, all he could think of was how funny his dad was! While he was drying his body off, his mind reflected back on his dream and the only thing that came to his mind was to hell with that dream!

The Haynes all went outside on the lawn. Ralph, Alma, and Annie Bell sat under that huge tree. The rest of the children were all running around playing tag and enjoying the moment. The weather was changing causing easy breathing and the wind would blow softly across the children's faces and their clothes would move like they were a part of the wind blowing in midair.

Chapter 9
Wedding Bells

Christmas came on in bright lights as always and it should always be remembered for its true meaning. On Christmas day all of Terry Hardy's families and friends were all invited to his lovely home. It was treated as a blessing in the Hardy family. The love of the families and friends were what the Hardy family was about. Annie Marie (Marilyn Hardy sister) wouldn't be anywhere else for the holiday. Annie Marie was accommodated by her son and close friend, Minister O'Brian. Mark Child, who is one of Terry Hardy's friends, was setting the mood for Christmas with his family and best friend, the harmonica.

Thomas Pain and his family were there to share the spirit of Christmas. The two boys were delighted to play together. The mistletoe, the fresh smell of pine and the lovely setting of the table set the mood for a sparkling blissful day. Marilyn Hardy had plenty of help with preparing the meal and it was well appreciated. Everyone thought it was worth the wait as they took their places at the table.

Alexander was home from college for Christmas, surrounded by his loved ones for a Christmas Feast. His fiancée was there just glowing and very happy. The two brothers, Michael and Herbert Tucker and their family were there. Guy Martin and his wife wouldn't have missed it for the world. Then Ralph and family entered the home and magically, everything got merrier.

Everyone was pleased as they greeted one another. Guy and his wife were playing the piano, and everyone joined in singing Christmas Carols. The singing automatically puts everyone in the spirit of Christmas. They were singing, while Alexander and Frances were setting the table for a fabulous meal. Then everyone was seated at the table and the children had their own personal table. They all showed their love and were pleased to celebrate the birth of Christ.

The timing was more than perfect. At the same time, the Hardy's family and Alexander's family homes prayers were in conformity. This was the Christmas that would go down in history. Merry Christmas!

In the year of 1928, Alexander's plans were to succeed at Jackson State College. Alexander was floating through the whole year.

His associates kept asking him, what was he taking, or they asked what was he on? They would ask questions because they wanted some of that too. Alexander had heard those words so many times, his responses came instantly as he spoke, "Uh,

Uh, Uh, I'm high off the higher of love, haven't you heard."

They would leave him alone for a while before starting at it again. In the meantime, he would get some much-needed work done. That's how Alexander got his well, deserved grades. He knew exactly what it took if he wanted to accomplish anything in life. His family had set a great example that has been displayed for him to follow. Luckily enough, he had the sense to aim for the better things in life. Alexander managed to stay out of trouble, and he was his own best friend. He knew that trouble was easy to adhere to in life. It was enticing as well as it being exciting. But there's all this negativity involved when you're trying to get out of messy situations.

Alexander worked hard and, in the end, it paid off. He received a Bachelor of Arts degree in Science and Economics at the end of that school term. In the month of May, he took all of it in with passion. It was the graduation that put that hum in his voice. It minted a new beginning for Alexander and to fit the occasion, the family invited their friends to a restaurant in Jackson afterward. There were twelve people in all, setting around two tables.

Guy Martin wouldn't miss this, even if someone were holding him for ransom. He would have made the great escape to be in the same atmosphere. Especially when this is such an important day and Michael Tucker felt the same way.
If Guy Martin was there, you should know that Michael and Herbert were there also. They all came together in love and

supported and celebrated their friend who had accomplished one of his dreams.

Herbert couldn't imagine anything else that could remotely be better than being a part of this. Michael stated, "There is nowhere I would like to be right now," then he threw his hands up and said, "That's why I'm here." There was laughter that filled the room.

Everyone had something to say, and everyone was excited because Alexander graduated. The clicking of the glasses as everyone made their speech. He was astonished with every click, and every word sounded wonderful to Alexander's ears as he smiled. The food was extremely pleasing to the taste. Alexander saw what he needed to see the most. As he gazed in the direction where his parents were seating and all he could see was loving pride. He acknowledged the love that was before him, and it made him feel that it was a necessary love for him to witness. He knew this was the kind of love that helped him succeed. Alexander had the right tools and he used them to his advantage.

Frances Carter was proud of the man she had fallen in love with. She gave a toast to the man she loved and wanted the world to know that she loved him and for certain ones to know to keep their hands off. Mother Alexander put her hand up to her mouth as she snickered after hearing the toast. She thought Frances was the perfect woman for her son. Mrs. Alexander stared into the young faces that shared such wonderful words of love. She knew there would be nothing but good in store in the future for the two.

This was a day to be remembered and you can believe they put their signature on this promising day. Alexander thanked everyone for sharing this moment of life with him and his family. As the Alexanders were departing, you could feel the warmth and his friends seemed to be rewarded by being his friend.

Now Frances had an excellent chance of spending time with her fiancé. She expressed herself in many ways on their way home. She wanted him to know that they had always talked about what it would be like living in another state. Frances questioned Alexander if he thought they could live a wonderful life here in Mississippi too, if they really tried.

Alexander looked at her with this unforgettable smile that expressed a thousand words. He wanted her to know, he would live anywhere as long as she was there with him. He knew they would do well here. Alexander enjoyed helping others and he could set an example by using himself to show others that we can do better for ourselves. "We should never give up and we need to help one another. But we can't help one another until we do something for us. That way we will be able to help someone else and really be sincere about it. In other words, people need to be able to give without needing it themselves."

Frances showed her honey that she comprehends what he was saying, "In other words we need to empower ourselves."

Frances looked into Alexander's eyes, and gathered from what he had just said, that we are not moving out of Mississippi, letting her know that statement was a green light.

Alexander believed they will do exceptionally well anywhere they live so they decided to do it right here in Mississippi. They wanted to spread their wings.

Frances knew she had planted that seed and the results were to her liking and to his as well. She wanted to be wherever Alexander was and to be near her family. Frances had this expression on her face but without speaking it, then she screamed, "Yeah."

Then Alexander stated, "Before you know it, we could start looking like one another."

Frances responded, "Baby I could wake up one morning and there and behold my nose could be looking like your nose. Yes, we could end up with each other's body parts. That would be something, huh honey?"

Alexander answered, "No, you are something," as he looked into her eyes, saying how funny this is, then he kissed her. After Alexander kissed her, he stated, "Since you wanted to go there, I would guess one morning when I woke up, I could have grown your breasts on my chest. How do you think I would look with breasts? Yeah breasts, all the way up to the neck."

Frances laughed while punching him on his arm. They rode around just enjoying the natural beauty of that wonderful day. It was nothing fancy, just sharing time with each other.

Time that was respected because they thought time was most important in how it is shared, and they ended the day at home together.

Saturday morning, May 26, 1928, never looked as beautiful as it looked that day. Frances and Alexander had been extremely busy, putting their plan into action. Today they decided to try it out with some of their friends. They invited their friends to Alexander's parents' home to be there for 3:00 p.m. As the time moved closer to three, Frances was staring out of the window looking over the backyard at all of their Families and friends, which she found to be quite entertaining to watch.

She recognized Mark Child and Terry Hardy with his family. Then her mind had drifted off to a place that wasn't a pleasant thought until she heard a voice that called her name. When she looked around, there stood her father, Mr. Carter, asking her, "Are you ready sweetheart?"

Frances was relieved to see her father as she responded to him, "Of course daddy," as she gave him a kiss on his cheek, and they embraced.

Her father spoke to her in a calm voice letting her know everything is going to be alright. "Now let's go and make something happen." Mr. Carter walked with his arm around Frances until they reached the back door. He told her that he loved her, and she never looked lovelier. They started walking side by side out of the door. All you could hear was the ooh and awe, as they walked down the aisle. Then Mr. Carter gave his only daughter away to Mr. A. A. Alexander to be wed.

They both looked amazing, but Alexander seemed a bit nervous until he looked into her hazel eyes. That's when he said his vows, he was completely focused, and that nervousness was all over. After they kissed, Frances held up her dress with one hand and they jumped over the broomstick. Then she threw her bouquet in the mix of many excited women. The music started and they danced, soon afterward others followed.

Alexander delightfully placed his hand on her hand as he assisted her at cutting the cake. Frances started first with a chuck of cake heading for his mouth in a hurry and he paid her back forward. For some, it brought back memories and for others they just wish to be next. Just as soon as everyone was relaxed into it all, Mr. and Mrs. Alexander drove off on their honeymoon. No one knew where the couple was going or that they had left, it was their secret honeymoon.

After about an hour had passed, everyone was feeling quite happy, even though the bride and groom had skipped town. They were headed north laughing and all snuggled up. Frances couldn't wait any longer, but Alexander already knew. He pulled into this fabulous place, and they got out and unlocked the door and then Alexander kicked it closed as he carried his bride into the bedroom. He started helping her to undress and got in the bed. Frances started dancing as she wiggled her hips as they were in a trance of their own. Alexander loved every minute of it as Frances joined her husband in the bed.

Frances took a deep breath and exhaled out the words, "We did it, we are married now, and you are my husband," as they made love like never before. She's Mrs. A. A. Alexander and feeling amazing. Frances felt wonderful, and that feeling had to be the reason so many people got married. Alexander was truly dedicated to Frances; he made her feel as if his name were meant for her and in his mind, no other human being could duplicate her. They were in paradise for a week before they made it back to Alexander's home.

As they were driving into the driveway of their home, Frances's mind was so in tune with where her home was now. She smiled because Alexander's home is where she lived, for now. Alexander opened the car door and held out his hand and Frances sprang out of the car into his strong arms like a wild kitten. Frances could sense the love from him, and she knew his love was the real deal. They stayed there silently without any disturbance.

A week later Mr. and Mrs. Alexander were ready to claim their friends again after spending needed time for themselves. Together they feel they would conquer the world. Adjusting to that feeling they visited their parents first. They had to let them know they were back and safe. Their parents were content knowing they were extremely happy in love.

While they were in Brookhaven, they drove to an area called Siloam. There they visited the two military brothers, Michael and Herbert. They all met at Michael and his wife

Mona's home. They were sitting around and seriously waiting to hear how they felt now that they're married. Mona could hardly wait, it could be either one, just as long as one of them spoke up.

Frances wanted to speak for the both of them as she looked at her husband. They both were smiling and gazing into each other's eyes. Frances started with, "First of all my friends we were already friends for quite a while. He was crazy about me. Right then I knew it was just a matter of time…," she leaned forward, "when I knew he would be all mine"

Everyone was so happy to hear it because they had nothing but love for them. Everyone was happy except for Mary, the wife of Herbert Tucker. Frances noticed that spark wasn't present on her face; there was something different about her.

Mary noticed that she had drawn unwanted attention as she began to explain, "It must be a bug or something, I'm sure that's all it could be." She didn't realize how she felt had become transparent. Frances assured her that the wonderful husband she has will keep an eye on her.

Herbert didn't have any problem with that statement as a matter of fact he let it be known how Mary and their child were his first priority. Not only that but how he will keep, not just one but both eyes on her. He smiled, as he placed his arm around her so gently like he does, most of the time anyway. "Family comes first in my book and that's for real!" said Herbert.

Herbert reached over and stroked her cheek, ever so gently with the back of his hand. Mary looked up at him with a sexy smile and seemed excited. They all had a great time catching up with each other. The newlyweds also got to spend some time with the Tuckers' precious children. They thought the children were actually the reason the Tucker family was as strong as they were. They sat outside on the porch and watched the three children dance a jig and then they played hide and seek. One would count while the other two hid. When one was found, his little legs looked as if they were a small wheel spinning trying to get to the base first. The grownups were cheering them on as they had tears rolling down their faces, as they watched with the expression of pure happiness.

Through those tears of joy in Michael's eyes, he saw Guy Martin parking in front of his home. Guy joined in with his friends and gave the married couple his blessing. He also suggested they have the blessing of having many, beautiful children. Guy stated, "My wife and I haven't been fortunate enough to bear any children, so far." He was silent for a moment after that with his head tilted. His eyes were the shade of green. His face was bright, with light freckles that covered his unique face. His hair was black and naturally curly, not to leave out that slim built body that gave him a certain distinguished look.

Frances thanked Guy and let him know they appreciate that lovely gesture about having kids. They will do just that when they decide on having children. The both of them understood and most of all they heard him. Frances reminded him, how that will come to pass, and it will be in their flavor. She spread her arms out to all of them because she wanted everyone to know it is so fortunate to have such friends who care about each other as they have done. Saying those words, "I thought my husband was going to call you guys to visit; while we were on our honeymoon, and it was kind of scary there for a moment."

"No!" That was the first word that came out of the mouths of the majority of everyone.

Mona, Michael's wife, responded that, "The men probably would have come, believe me." Guy had a little problem with that, he was thinking along the lines of they would discuss it first. The women had a reasonable disagreement telling the men they were killing them with that nonsense.

Mona brought the children in to take a bath and relax. Mary insisted on helping, it would take less time with the two of them. After all, one of the children belonged to her. Frances assured them they would still be there when they returned. She wouldn't be able to drag her husband away from them right now anyway.

Guy started talking about a meeting that he had attended in the downtown area. Everyone wanted to know what was going on in the meeting as they were looking around at each other. They were thinking, is he still claiming that he's attending the "White People meeting." He had forever and always told them about meetings that he attended. That they were important meetings and were just as interesting.

Frances stopped talking; she just stared at Guy as if it

were her first time seeing him. Frances expressed a full smile and started gazing into Guy's eyes. Then everyone started staring at Frances. Alexander reached for Frances demanding to know what was happening with her and what she saw. Guy decided to compliment her eyes while she was staring, and she thanked him. "But the million-dollar question is why are you staring into my eyes, what do you see?" Guy questioned.

Frances was elated then she called Guy by his full name. "Guy Martin, you little devil you I see an excellent profile of a white man. We have known you for so long, we didn't pay attention to that being a possibility, we missed it. You were not afraid, attending those meetings by yourself at all?"

Guy responded, "What I got to be afraid of, I'm a man like all the rest of them."

The rest of the men joined in, and everyone was talking at the same time. Herbert was impressed he never had a clue and he had to admit, Guy had a great disguised advantage working for him. Everybody thought that he was making up some tall tales and some real good ones too. Now it all makes sense. Herbert shook his hand while telling Guy, "You are my kind of man for a little man in sizes with a huge heart. As they all joined in, shaking his hand repeating, 'good job.' They all were laughing as Mary and Mona were entering the room.

"By now the kids were all in their sleep world with the angels," Mona said. They made refreshments for everyone, as they set the trays with drinks on the table, and they served themselves. Mary sensed they had missed something stimulating as they joined in on the conversation. Frances filled the two in on what was discovered. Guy was receiving information that was golden. He knew people had doubts about him, but he knew what he was saying came right out of the horse's mouth, whether they believe him or not.

At this moment, he was a happy soul. He can't explain it, but he loved how he was feeling. Herbert suggested that they make a toast and they all said, "Yeah, together."

Herbert raised his glass and said, "Friends forever!" They all repeated the same as their glasses clicked as they touched.

Herbert knew one thing about Guy, "He is smart, and honest. If you don't want to know the truth, please don't ask Guy. You know I think he would be a damn good detective. Even though he would probably need to stay undercover to keep from being killed. You know, sometimes honesty is not always a good policy."

Mary thought about someone she knew who could fill that pitcher to its capacity. She turned to face Herbert and spoke about how funny that was for him to say that because he would fight the same way for his rights. He knows he wouldn't have it any other way. "It's those simple and pure things that we do and if you tossed that in a bowl and you stir it all up. When you pour the mix, it turns out to be Guy Martin as a result. But I know we all have that same quality, that's why we are all linked here together," and they all said, "Here, here."

Guy made a complement that fitted them all about owning that natural high about them. They all came together with all of this uniqueness about all of them. "So, you know, that makes them automatically stand out o.k." Guy Martin knew what will take everybody's mind to a higher place. He had it right there with him. Then he pulled out of his pocket a deck of cards.

That's when Alexander looked at him from the corner of his eyes and tilted his hat and said, "I'm ready partner." Everyone was excited and sworn that they were the one who was going to kick the other one's butt. That night ended in the fun of the card games and their high spirit brought out the best of it.

Chapter 10
The Love of My Life

It was a Saturday morning, the ninth of June 1928. Michael was up early and out the door, headed to his car. Herbert was not far behind him as they both drove off together. Michael told Herbert, "How driving in the morning has this magical feeling about it, like no other time of the day. It's the best time to be on the road. The air smelled different, it smelled clean. It makes you feel if anything were ailing you, just by taking long deep breath you would be cured. Then the sun started smiling on you from out of nowhere."

Herbert agreed, "It has that Godly feel about it. You know there's something powerful about it. We have all of this beauty around us, and we never think about how much power it represents but man that's some powerful stuff."

Michael noticed his big brother liked talking about nature. But Herbert made it clear that there were times when that was all he could do was lay back watching the stars. Now it may sound crazy but then, there was nothing crazy about it. He was there for Uncle Sam and gave it his all; but watching those stars became therapy for Herbert and it was welcome, appreciated and needed. Herbert was sloped in his seat listening to his little brother and he agreed, "I have no problem with nature."

They reached their designation and Michael parked in front of the South Side Meat Market. They entered saying good morning. Terry was there and welcomed them into the market. He knew they couldn't stay away for long. Terry smiled as he wanted to know what he could do for them, they laughed.

The brothers were generous in choosing their meats. Terry was very talkative as he worked his way of putting extra weight on the scale with his magic finger. They didn't notice the quick finger of Terry, just his fresh farm meat. Afterwards, they make it home very pleased with their choices of meats.

Herbert went straight to his kitchen and prepared breakfast for Mary and their son, Chris. He surprised Mary by serving her breakfast in bed. Herbert enjoyed doing little things for her just to see her smile. But now Mary wasn't feeling her best as she smiled while he fed her.

After a couple of days had passed Mary was feeling better which gave Herbert a great idea for his family to do. As he prepared the vehicle with his wife and son, he began thinking about how he loved them and how important they are to him. He came to a long road where all you could see were trees and roads. It looked as if the trees were protecting the road. They parked on Herbert's private piece of land that was breathtaking. Chris was so excited he got out of the vehicle to help his dad. Together they placed a blanket in a beautiful spot and Herbert set the basket on a small stand beside it. Mary was lying on her back with her head on Herbert's lap.

The butterflies were huge, beautiful, and colorfully, they were all over the place. The butterflies could not get enough of all of those unique, wildflowers with the mixture of their fragrance. Chris loved all of that natural entertainment that nature provided. Herbert and Mary watched Chris being captivated by the bugs' beauty and he couldn't stop playing with them. There was a stream of water that ran from a lake that made a waterfall into a beautiful running stream. It was so peaceful; Mary kept a smile on her face the whole time they were there.

Mary started playing with Chris. Herbert thought "She's smiling, look how beautiful she is." He saw a radiant of light from the sun shining through the trees that gently touched her face. She wore a baby blue cotton dress that took Herbert back to a great time they had together, while she was playing with their son. All three of them looked like a photo in a silver frame. He shouted enthusiastically, "I'm blessed, and yes, there is a God." Mary reached for Chris' hand as they ran to Herbert with their open arms as they plunged to the ground in laughter. Herbert took Chris hand and started stroking his head. He wanted his loved ones to know this was one of those exciting moments.

Herbert watched the event he planned bloom before his

eyes, turning out to be better than what he expected. "Honey, I know you remember the saying, heaven is right here on earth," Herbert stated?

Mary was staring him right in his eyes, "Of course."

Herbert finished, "There are places that would make you think of that phrase, and this happens to be one of those places." They were there together, in their secret paradise and that was all that mattered to Mary. She wouldn't want to be with anyone else other than her two men, that she loved more than life itself.

Chris loved his mom, and he knew she wasn't feeling well but to see her smiling was well worth it all in this wonderful surrounding which was so peaceful. He could not take it any longer. He had to ask his mom if she was feeling better?

Mary didn't want her son to think, for one minute, that his mom didn't feel like being there for him. So naturally her response was to shoot straight to the heart as she embraced him. She said, "Every day, I wake up and you are in my presence, I'm in heaven and every breath I take, you are near me and guess what?"

Chris answered, "What mom?"

Mary responded, "I'm in heaven. Babe, I love you. You are this huge star that shined through me. It's the light of your future. This light is what I use to guide you with because this light is you, shining with me all the way. If there's a time you don't see me, I want you to know that I'm that light of yours. I will always be there."

Herbert got up and reached his hand out to help them up, whispering to Mary, "What you said to Chris was beautiful, his face even lit up while you were talking to him." Herbert felt spectacular listening to her as she reassured their son.

Herbert took some plastic paper off half a watermelon. The watermelon rind was cut in a zigzag style around the edges. It was loaded with fruits, berries, and other delicious treats for his family. Herbert planned every moment to be the finest and that made him feel complete and loved all over. That's what it felt like when they arrived until it was time to exit. The picnic was so beautiful, it was a shame to have to leave but it truly was rewarding. Herbert could not call it quits and go home, so they just rode around enjoying the scenery.

It was the 13th day of June, on a Wednesday morning, the wives and the kids were going to take Michael's vehicle on their day of adventure. It was Michael who was meeting Herbert today so they could get their hair cuts. Herbert tried to start his vehicle, but it wouldn't start and that led him to look under the hood. Michael told him; he didn't know what he was doing. Then Herbert told him to close his mouth and turn the key. Michael was surprised when he heard the engine kick off.

Right away, Herbert started laughing, jokingly asking Michael, "Did you hear something?" Herbert let the hood down, with his eyes on Michael pointing his finger while shaking his hand. Herbert got in his vehicle and said, "And-it's-what? I can't hear you now."

Michael was just sitting there laughing for a second when he suggested to Herbert that they need to be on their way. The barbershop didn't have as much as a crowd right then. That made the brothers able to get their haircuts and shaved at a more desirable pace and made it possible to get in and out quicker.

It was so quick they made it back home before the rest of the family did. The two just sat there in the driveway without getting out of the Ford vehicle. Then Herbert had this brilliant idea, he started up the car again and said, "I have an excellent place to take you." The two men were on their way to town when Herbert noticed he was nearing Marvin Towns' Auto Repair Shop where he had taken his battery to be charged. Herbert stopped to check on his battery that he had left there several weeks ago to be charged and each time he checked to pick it up, it still needed to be charged. Michael stayed in the car while Herbert went into the shop.

When he entered, Joe L. Hart was talking while leaning under the hood of a car. Joe was there most of the time just to have something to do, mainly wasting time. Marvin Towns looked over toward the door as Herbert was walking in and asked Herbert if he needed to see him. When he said that Joe Hart told Marvin, he would see him later and he left.

Herbert proceeded talking, telling Marvin that he stopped to pick up his battery that's setting up in here (as he pointed to it). Marvin Towns let him know then that his battery hadn't been charged yet because he had been busy. Marvin started tightening up a bolt under the hood of the car that he was working on. Herbert knew what was happening and he responded, "You meant for it to be inconvenient but most of all it's disappointing for anyone to have to go through something as crazy as this. I have served in the military maybe like you have also. I'm not asking you to give me something for free, this is something I would have to pay for, is this stupid or what. But right now, I'm concerned about my battery, and you know why my battery isn't charged."

"Next time, it will be ready," comes from the voice of Marvin Towns. He rises up from leaning under the hood of the car, motioning his hand with a pair of pliers in it. He told Herbert when he comes back his battery will be ready.

"Until then you have my battery ready." That was Herbert's last remark. Herbert exited out of the door and went back to his car telling Michael, "Let's move far away from here, man my battery was sitting in there as usual."

Michael agrees, "Yes let's haul ass, I'm ready for whatever, and it's looking like a day to remember." Michael didn't have a clue of where Herbert was heading. Herbert drove into Royal Chevrolet's car lot; that's when Herbert suggested he could use a new car. "For real," Michael replied.

Herbert looked over at Michael saying, "As you would say it, hell yeah." Herbert wanted to see what they could find, and he suggested they might need to check out more than one place. They got out of their vehicle and started picking out cars.

Herbert saw one car and said, "It looks like, it could be saying, 'take me, take me.' That one over there looks like it could be a female car, looking sassy and all. It's shouting, 'You know I'm the stuff take me.' Can you hear them talking Michael?

Michael responded," Hell yeah, that's how it gets you."

They both laughed for a minute. Then Herbert saw THE CAR, it was as if he heard angels singing from a far. He drove into the parking lot driving a Ford vehicle. A couple hours later, he drove off that parking lot driving a Chevrolet car and a fine one at that. It was a long day because Herbert drove a while, then Michael drove a while, to get the feel of it. They rode, laughed, and talked for hours, before they retired for the day.

By then the wives and kids made it home, there was even more joy riding because they were surprised by the new black Chevrolet car parked in the driveway. Michael was so excited talking about Herbert's car that Herbert had to ask them if he was still talking about his car. Michael went with Herbert to his home while their families were enjoying the drive in the new ride.

It was exactly one hundred and twenty minutes had passed when the telephone rang, and Herbert answered. Herbert looked at Michael and insisted they needed to go to the Hospital, "right now." Michael jumped up and they were on their way. Herbert explained to Michael the reason they were going to the hospital. When they entered the hospital, Mona was with the kids in the waiting room.

Michael immediately embraced Mona. Herbert embraced the children because they were upset. Mona looked at Herbert with sadness all over her face. She informed them that Mary's doctor reported that she had what was called Pneumonia. She let Herbert know where to go and Michael went along with him. Mary was in the Intensive Care Unit, and she wasn't looking well at all. She was looking very weak and when she spoke, her words were incoherent. Herbert nor Michael could believe that she was in such a state. Michael went to get his wife and their children, and they prayed outside of her room. Herbert prayed as he held their son.

"Oh Lord," Herbert moaned, "You are the reason we're united; you are the reason we have so much love and joy. "We need her," Herbert cried. "I won't know what to do if all of this we have were to stop right now my Lord. Please, Lord, keep blessing us. Lord, please answer our prayer but I know only you know best. Maybe you see the need for her right now and if that's so, we will manage to live with whatever you say. My Lord, but we really love her, and we want more than anything for her to be in this world, for her to stay in our life right now. Please Lord, answer our prayer, Amen."

They all were sobbing as Herbert asked them to keep their son tonight. Mona let him know, he didn't have to ask, it's already done. As Herbert hugged Chris, he told him not to worry, they will be home soon. They all were back and forth to the hospital and now it's on that fourth day. They could see a change in Mary for the first time since she had been in the hospital. Everyone was excited and waiting to hear how soon she will be returning home. Herbert knew today would not be the day for Mary to leave and he was there for that fifth night, Sunday June the 17 1928.

Monday morning, Herbert had awakened and all he could see was Nurses and as he looked a little closer there stood her doctor, Dr. Lampson was trying to revive her but there was no response from her having a massive heart attack. Herbert stood up and he looked at Mary as tears started flowing down his brown sugar face. As he wiped each tear it was like a part of him went with each tear that he wiped, like melting sugar. He went to her, trying desperately to wake her up, as the tears were flowing profusely.

Dr. Lampson patted Herbert on his back saying, "I'm sorry, her sickness was too much for her." Michael was there soon afterward with the rest of the families. Everyone filled the room. Then the prayer came, and it was hard for the family to see Mary's body being taken away. They were still standing there, crying in disbelief.

Michael knew everyone needed to be vacating this area, he assisted everyone out of the room and that wasn't a pleasant sight. With all of them, pulling together they had enough strength to manage to make it home in peace. Their life had changed, that's all they could feel for now. The change didn't feel like change for the better. Death greets us all the time, but we never feel that it should be welcome. The flow of death moves within us cutting in a zigzag style. It leaves a permanent scar, inside and out. We do what we can to get over this unwanted feeling that never feels right.

Chapter 11
Mary's Funeral

They had to work through this feeling. Herbert, Michael, and Mona worked the arrangement so that the funeral would be as swift as possible. The funeral was Thursday June 21, 1928. The weather is always warm this time of the year. Their plan was to be done with the funeral before temperatures became unbearable. The funeral was at Siloam Church. The weather was cool and there was a breeze that came with it, the timing was great.

The funeral started at 11:00a.m, but it still didn't matter because that was the worst day ever for the Tucker family. Right before anyone's emotions got out of control, their friends were there for them. They could walk out from the church on the grave site. As Herbert stood in front of Mary's grave, he watched her casket being lowered into the ground. He didn't hear anything that was said, he just felt that he was right there with her. He wanted her to feel that he would take care of everything, and their love goes on for eternity.

Michael and Mona stayed close to Chris and Herbert, until the casket was lowered and covered. Soon afterward their friends left, so they could share their needed private time with Mary. Then Herbert was standing alone staring at Mary's grave as if he was looking right at her.

Herbert squatted as he talked to Mary about their son, how he will be taken care of and that she will never have to worry. Then he made a fist and hit his chest with it, "The love you shared with us is locked right here." He stood and his eyes were filled with tears and sadness. He felt that he had lost the most important thing that was keeping him alive. Then Chris walked up to him and grabbed this leg. Herbert reached down and picked him up and they embraced each other. Right then his heart wasn't empty anymore. He realized that he wasn't alone, and he wasn't the only one who was hurting.

Recognizing this pulled Herbert closer to the rest of the family. When that happened, the healing began but this time all of them were included. Everyone was feeling strange and empty. They reached their home with hardly a word exchange. Herbert took Chris to change their clothes so they could be more comfortable. Herbert wanted to stay close to him because he needed that tender toughness and being able to display those to Chris would be great for Herbert's well-being also.

Michael helped Mona with the children so they could be content. Then Michael gave Mona a hug that lifted her off the floor. She whispers, "I love you more than you know."

No sooner than she whispered those words Michael came back with, "I know my love," as he fastened his lips upon her earlobe, Mona smiled knowing that her husband was hurting also. Then he lowered her to the floor, he told Mona as soon as they change their clothes, Herbert and Chris will be over and we will all be here altogether.

"We will be around each other until we get ourselves together and I know you will love that. The children and I will love that as well. So, let's get ready and make ourselves feel alive and I know you are all for that and Mary as she rests in peace, as well." Michael embraced her and she seemed to be calm and pleased as he accommodated her as they got dressed.

June 24, 1928, Herbert opened his big brown eyes to a beautiful Sunday morning. Lying there for about a minute after he had awakened, he realized he wasn't alone. There seemed to be another soul lying beside him, as he slowly turned his head to see what it was and to his surprise he was exhilarated because what he saw was his son Chris. Herbert knew Chris had to be afraid to sleep alone but he still made that attempt. Chris would fall asleep in his bed, but he would awaken and that's when he would make that move straight to his dad's bed to sleep. Herbert just watched Chris as he slept. He could imagine what an angel must look like watching him sleep.

Chris was soon awake, and Herbert wanted to ask him how he was feeling and if he was up to attending church this morning? By Chris being the little man that he portrayed, the answer was, "Yes Daddy I like going to church." They were invited by a friend to visit his church, Herbert and Michael accepted. Both of them knew they would feel better just being there.

When they arrived, Reverend Ned Owens at Friendship Church took them to that setting in another time zone and then he walked them through it. Rev. Owens was one of those gifted Reverend's who kept himself intact, reaching and moving in an ascending position. He loved seeing his members enjoying and responding with excitement.

Rev. Owens preached with ease, and he reached out to others with helping hands. All three of the children got up and took a long stretch after church was over. The members of the church, who saw the children stretching, got a good laugh as everyone was mingling and shaking the Reverend's hand. Some of the members were headed toward the kitchen where there had to be some good food nearby. There were several sister's serving the food. Everyone was requesting exactly what they wanted. That process made everyone move swiftly and on to the grounds outside.

Outside, there were boards that were placed close to each other. The boards went from one tree to another. That is where the plates were set. There were benches in front of the table where everyone sat comfortably. Michael kept watching one of the sisters because she kept going into the kitchen and coming back with a couple of plates. The sister was eating them almost as fast as she was going to get them. Herbert was talking to Rev. Owens about how it is so hard for all of them trying to cope with the thought of Mary's presence being nonexistent.

Mona expressed how it's definitely day by day reality for all of them right now. "There's times when certain things that happen that make you think about things, and you see them in a different light. It's like looking at a photograph to witness your loved one fading off of it but the love and the memory you have for that person remains in your heart forever." Mona tears were flowing profusely down her face as she tried to control herself.

Rev. Owens started praying right away to help release some of the pressure that was on their hearts. Each word the Reverend spoke, they felt the power that relieved pain. As soon as the Reverend finished praying there were sounds of intensity. Everyone turned around in the direction of that unpleasant sound. It was the sister that Michael was paying attention to, earlier. Michael realized that the noise maker was the sister who was eating two plates at a time. Everyone was looking around, the sister couldn't move or breathe, she was still sitting at the table.

Another church member ran into the church and found a pair of scissors to help assist the sister with some relief. She started cutting, first the dress then the girdle. Then the lady that was in distress, daughter started screaming, "No---- don't cut that girdle, I just bought that girdle! I paid good money for that girdle! No----!" The sister kept cutting, soon after she finished cutting her girdle. The sister removed the girdle right away.

Then all of a sudden, there was a loud buff sound, "Old Lord" cried the sister who cut the girdle.

Unfortunately, the lady had consumed too much food and her stomach expanded like an inflated balloon. The good out of this is, she still had her dress on and that was a blessing because she had everyone's attention now. But the show had come to an end.

Mona looked at Michael and Herbert as she was trying to express how attending church today somehow had this mysterious kind of effect on all of them. Who would have thought it would end like this. It's like there's an intervention happening at all times and frankly she was feeling better now because of that. Now they were ready to go home. Mona thanked Reverend Owens for making them feel like humans again. Reverend Owens promised that he would keep them in his prayers and his visits would be frequent. He didn't want them to worry about anything. He embraced each one of them with a blessing.

Michael was glad to see home again and the same was true for them all. Chris wanted to stay over with Todd and Jasper, and Mona agreed for Chris to stay as long as he didn't get sick for his dad, we can handle the rest. Herbert agreed with Mona; they will see what happens or how long it will last.

Later that day, Ralph Haynes, A. A. Alexander, and Guy Martin were standing on the front porch of Michael's home.

There was a knocking at the door and Herbert answered it with pleasure and he welcomed his friends into the home as they embraced each other. Mona explained how having everyone over makes a difference and for them to keep coming. Herbert felt loved. Michael was impressed by their friends because they had brought food with them too.

Alexander explained that he had stopped by Terry Hardy's meat market, and he sent packages of fresh meat. Herbert thought that was nice as they took the food to the kitchen, and they played several hands of Bid Whist. While the children played in their bedroom with their toys, there was some laughter again, great food, and plenty to drink. That lasted for many hours and Mona admitted she had a day of normalcy.

It felt good but there is another part of her that comes out that reminds her that she's not there yet and it takes over her emotions. Michael put his arms around her, and he just stood there holding her, rocking her from one side to the other. Michael reminded her that they all are in the same boat, "That's why we're all here together. Things will get better but in its own time, in its own time, honey, it will happen," Michael whispered.

Herbert gave all three of the children a hug and a kiss. Herbert stressed the words "Be good" to the children.

Todd and Jasper said, "Yes Uncle Herbert, we will."

Chris gave his dad another hug; then his dad gave Mona a hug while whispering, to promise to let him know if she needed him, he will be at home because he needs some extra rest. It felt like a ton of bricks was sitting on his shoulders, so Herbert headed home.

Herbert was tense and it was difficult trying to relax so he kept busy. He started thinking about how being active in this life has always helped him and began doing sit-ups. Herbert also knew this was the best and healthiest way he knew to relieve stress other than being with his other half, the love of his beautiful wife. He knew his emotions would be on an overload. Herbert never thought he would be without Mary. He never thought of her dying. He felt the loneliness that screamed with pain for his Mary, like never before. It was a feeling he knew would always be there.

Herbert wasn't exercising anymore, after doing over a hundred sit-ups and push-ups. He was lying flat on his back, staring at the ceiling. After falling asleep on the floor, he decided to take a warm bath and relax for the rest of the night.

In Mona's home, Michael helped her put Jasper, Todd, and Chris to bed. Mona couldn't wait to be alone with her husband and at last they were finally alone. After Michael finished taking his bath, he fixed some more bath water and Mona held Michael's hand as she stepped into the tub of warm water.

Michael wrapped his muscular arms around Mona, and she was leaning back on his hairy chest that cushioned her with comfort. He placed his lips to her ear and whispered how special and wonderful she is and how she has brought those emotions out in their life. She responded with a kiss and Michael started bathing her. He started with her face, washing her in a small circling motion just like you would bath a baby. He his way all the way down to her kissable toes.

As Mona stepped out of the tub, Michael wrapped her with a fresh off the line cloth. She could even feel the breeze, as he carried her into their bedroom. This treatment couldn't get any better as they kissed their way into the greatest love to be made. Michael whispered Mona's name saying, "I'm so lucky to have you in my life."

Chapter 12
The Troubles of the World

A week after Mary's death, her spirit had to be present, watching her loved ones, lifting their hearts, and embracing them. The seriousness that comes with this thing called death is the sadness, fear, emptiness, and the feeling of giving up. Death will seriously take those circumstances to its deepest level. Because the brothers lived on the same street, it was easy for Mona to get the kids and prepare a hot meal for everyone. Not only did they live next to each other, the two brothers worked for the same company.

The company they worked for was called Willard Commodity; it was located in the downtown area of Brookhaven. Willard Commodity was open Monday through Saturday, and they are there from 8:00 a.m. to 5:00 p.m. The Brothers work as Porters, the company was located in front of the train station. They meant business and strictly business when it came to their occupation.

They handled the incoming merchandise at the store but when the train arrived, they would help the passengers with their baggage and get it on and off the train. They enjoyed their jobs. They were meeting people every day and the atmosphere, of it all, suited their outgoing behavior, not to mention the tips that they received while they were working. That was an average workday for the Tucker Brothers.

Friday morning, Herbert had parked his Chevrolet car, west of S. M. Sawyer's Store in the parking lot. It was around 9:30 a.m. on the 29th of June, when Otis Smith spotted Herbert. Otis had blond hair that he wore pulled back in a ponytail and a low-cut beard. Otis approached Herbert asking for a payment that was due to him for months. It was the amount of six dollars, for his service on his Ford car. Herbert explained that he had traded in his Ford car as a down payment on the Chevrolet car that he was driving proudly.

Herbert didn't make any comment concerning how he was going to pay or any agreement at all as to what he was intended to do about that particular matter. Herbert was acting bold in behavior and blameless. But Herbert did say that he would see about it when he came back and left Otis standing there. Then Otis yelled out, "I'll be standing here when you get back." Herbert walked off leaving his car parked in the parking place.

That's how the situation was stated from the white's neighborhood but in the black's neighborhood the situation was stated that, "Herbert had taken his battery to be charged at Otis Repair Shop and that incident had taken place months ago. Every time Herbert attempted to pick up his battery at Otis Repair Shop, Otis would fail to have it charged. The problem was about having a battery charged and the story continued.

After Herbert had walked off and left his car in the parking lot, Otis had a partner who was occupying part of the shop. Robert E. Holmes was the occupant of Otis Smith Repair Shop. Robert (the occupant) came out of the shop and because Herbert had an account due to Otis, he decided for Holmes to go to Royal Chevrolet to "corroborate what the Negro had said." After Robert E. Holmes had wheeled off, about forty-minutes had passed before Herbert Tucker returned to the parking area. No one saw him when he eased into his vehicle, and he managed to get in it and was driving off. But Otis was on top of the game. He started running and caught up with Herbert in his vehicle.

Otis jumped on the running board of the car and reached in turning the steering wheel and the car landed in another parking lot. After Otis did that, Herbert Tucker release what was on his mind to Smith saying, "I can't see paying any mother fucking white man anything, I don't want to and you are not going to get a mother fucking cent, you mother fucker."

Otis balled up his fist and started hitting Herbert in his face. As that was taking place, his brother Michael drove up with their brother-in-law, beside him. They both were in one of Willard's Commodity Trucks.

Otis's brother, Eugene Smith, who happened to be getting his mail, was on his way back to Otis's shop, east of the railroad. From a hundred feet away, Eugene saw what was happening. He grabbed a shovel from the shop and started running from the south corner. Herbert Tucker had managed to get out of his car and struck Otis down with a full length, force hit, upside Otis's head.

Eugene reached the scene and he hit Herbert upside his head with the flat side of the spade. Then Michael got out of the truck with his gun. He fired, hitting Eugene Smith in the shoulder and the second shot shattered the bone in one leg. The shot went through, piercing the other leg, and then Eugene dropped, unable to rise. There was a car between Michael and Eugene.

Michael Tucker turned and fired point blank at the face of Eugene. He had his eyes on Michael Tucker and quickly dropped behind the car and the bullet missed him. There was a barber shop nearby, the owner was Andy Howard and Corey McDaniel worked at the same place. The men were coming together to give Otis assistance and Michael shot at both of them, which gave Otis time to run. He ran down the street and entered into his Repair Shop. The Deputy Sheriff happened to be in the locality and fired once at Michael, then he ran straight out the back, then he reloaded.

Herbert was captured, after being hit in the head with a shovel, by the Deputy Sheriff and Sheriff Maxwell. There was a crowd gathering by now, with a subsequent hunt for Michael Tucker. There was much excitement as the crowd grew. Minutes later two men were calling for help in the chase after Michael. They were on West Monticello Street when Michael Tucker came out of an entrance. They asked if he was the man who was wanted and was in the fight. They said that Michael was denying being the one, but he pulled out his pistol into one of the men's stomachs and enforced his command to be left alone. Then he ran east toward the railroad. When Michael was about to be overtaken, he would continuously run then turn and fire. But Michael only had one gun.

It looked like a hundred had joined in by now, including the Sheriff, the Chief of Police, a former Chief, and citizens. There was a range of shooting that failed to stop Michael Tucker. When Michael reached the railroad, he turned and ran near the Cotton Oil Mill. Several persons started to fight him off but were dissuaded by the sight of the automatic pistol he was firing. He didn't stop until he reached the south side.

Michael was seen going into a house where he took refuge, he had reached his home. Then the officers and the citizens started closing in. They looked all through the house. They believed that Michael was in the closet. So, they searched the entire house except the closet. Then the Sheriff started pumping lead into the closet. There wasn't a sound afterward. Then his pistol fell through the crack of the closet door. Michael crumpled to the floor, the Lincoln County Times stated, "It was from weakness."

The officer had to protect their prisoner and it was with difficulty trying to proceed with achieving that from the crowd in the process of transferring him to the jail cell at that time. After Michael Tucker was jailed, the County Health Physician dressed his wounds. Although there were five bullet wounds, Dr. Washington pronounced him as not desperately hurt.

The ambulance was on its way to the scene where everything started, at the Lincoln Motel. There was a lot of confusion going on as far as the traffic was concerned. As the ambulance was traveling on West Monticello it was approaching the street crossing. There was a car that failed to observe the east and west stop signal, which almost caused a wreck by the driver of the ambulance. There was some damage done to the ambulance by running into the old concrete water trough in order to avert a car-to-car smash.

Then the ambulance was able to reach Otis and Eugene Smith, both of them were rushed to the hospital. Otis Smith was expected to be out today, but with Eugene it was uncertain to foretell the outcome. His wounds resulted in a serious condition.

There were rumors that accelerated about the Tucker brothers that at any time, they would be together when they did see Otis smith. The employee at the Hardware Store had stated, "Michael Tucker was just there right before the trouble started, trying to buy some cartridges and the employee refused to sell them to him." There wasn't enough time to fully investigate the statements. Rumors were freely being circulated.

After the Tucker brothers had been arrested, a couple of hours later Sheriff Maxwell felt that Teddy E. Smith, the brother-in-law of the Tucker brothers, was in on it too. So, the Deputy Sheriff arrested him and was holding him as an accomplice. In the afternoon, Sheriff Maxwell, feared that a mob would form, he could feel it. He was thinking of his prisoner and made an application to the Governor to send some troops, they will be well needed. But he was on a fishing trip near Shreveport, Louisiana and could not be located.

Then the Sheriff thought about his lawyer friend. He could have appealed to Judge G. E. Townsend but as for reinforcements, he did not get any relief. There was no stretch of imagination and the crowd continued to grow impenetrable, like thousands. Throughout the evening starting from the time of the fight, people spent part of or all of the evening viewing what was taking place. The crowd continued to grow larger and denser, enough to be at least 6,000 people; men, women, and children were gathered around the courthouse as it was meant to be or set up to be.

The Tucker brothers' friends were sick at how this happened and so quickly. Ralph Haynes, A. A. Alexander, and Guy Martin stayed at their homes for now and all they could do was pray.

Mona took the kids and went to her parents' home in town and stayed there. It was hard pretending to be calm while she was around the children. She wanted time for herself before having to explain to the children about what had happened. "Oh God, what will I do?" Mona cried as she was falling apart.

Terry Hardy left the meat market and went to see Mark Child to tell him what was happening. They were sitting in the front yard; Mark already had heard. He knew this didn't sound promising for the Tucker brothers and the way everything was looking it was going to be a horrific moment. Mark laid back on a bench in his yard and started blowing his harmonica singing "Troubles of the world will soon be over."

Terry just sat there beside Mark saying, "This can't be happening here and to someone we know."
Mark just kept blowing the harmonica and singing.

Sheriff Maxwell failed to secure relief to guard against a militia, which only added to the critical moment. Starting at dusk, there were pleas by several of the city's most highly respected and honorable citizens, Reverends, and others to let justice rule. Just as it was getting dark at 8:00, on the south side of the jail had the real active portion of the mob. There were probably three or four hundred at that point. Even in the dim light they played the role of at least a half of a hundred Winchesters and shotguns standing up and above the shoulders and heads of the men. All it took was somebody shouting, "Let's go! Let's go!" The cry was like magic, and the crowd moved forward surging to the jail door.

There was not a shot fired doing the hour the mobs

spent battering down the three steel jail doors. The mob had 8x8 timber ten feet long which they used to strike that door which was used repeatedly. Sheriff Maxwell had joined in to help, endeavoring to push back the timber which resulted in his left wrist being caught between the timber and the door. His arm was partly crippled, and it had to be dressed afterward. Then the law officer knew he could not save his prisoners.

Sheriff Maxwell pleaded with them while ten policemen including deputies were meeting the crowd at the door. Without a doubt, these officers made an effort toward pushing the crowd back without avail until the officers finally gave up hope.

Now the Tucker brothers were the mob's prisoners. The mob took their prisoners down from the upstairs cell. There was one shout that came out from those emerging from the door of the jail. All three men were in the steel cell together, but the mob did not hinder Teddy E. Smith (the brother –in-law of the Tucker brothers). As the mob took the brothers, their behavior was described as a manual operation. As if they were soldiers on drill duty, according to the Lincoln County Times. Michael and Herbert Tucker were marched into two separate cars. While those who were just looking on as sightseers could hardly realize what had occurred because of the swiftness of the emergence of the jail.

The mob that had taken the Tucker brothers a half a mile south on Highway 51. In the meantime, there were thirty vehicles which had been placed with their heads turned toward the south in order for that to happen. They were parked on the wrong side of the street so no one else could park there. They were in harmony with the words "Old Brook." As they started south, there were hundreds of vehicles, which were trailing along for blocks, moving slowly.

Herbert didn't hear anything that was said because his mind was on his family. It was as if his son was right there before him. Watching Chris play with his mother, Mary, and the entire thing they did was so clear right then. The love he was feeling, he was hoping that Chris knows that he loves him. His heart was bleeding with pain and there was no way humanly possible of him having the chance to fight now. Then the car stopped.

They had reached their destination. "Until the Negroes were dead there would be no shooting;" those were the rules. It was bright out with all of the cars' headlights. A rope was attached to Herbert's neck and the other end was being thrown over a tree limb. There were willing hands to help; Herbert was being dragged in the sight of his brother's eyes. A few minutes afterwards, volley and volley were fired.

Michael was standing there barely, with five bullets wound from the morning fight, and then all eyes fell on him. They turned around with Michael, who had a rope around his neck, and they headed back to Brookhaven. Michael had a lot to digest, and his time was limited. He was in a bad place and was not going anywhere on his own. As the mob entered into the city Michael shouted, "So..be...it, you mother fuckers!"

After the vehicle stopped, Michael was pulled out of the vehicle by the rope and tied to the axle of the truck. According to the Lincoln County newspaper he was dragged by persons unknown around the street. (According to the Black neighborhood, there was a black male driving the vehicle). He attempted to jump on the back of the vehicle, but he was kicked off. Michael was pulled block after block and through the Negro quarters. That proceeded for a half an hour or so, with Michael Tucker just dangling behind as they headed north on Highway 51, toward Wesson.

The truck was followed by a procession of other automobiles. Then they took a side road for a quarter of a mile until the mob reached a tree branch. That's where Michael Tucker's body, what was left of the mutilated body, was hung up on a tree limb and then he was excessively filled with bullets. The double lynching was considered as a classic and all orderly lynching. Both of the roads that were leading to the dangling bodies of the mob's victims were to be viewed at extremely offensive public displays. The crowd had gathered at the courthouse to see the lynching by following cars either to Old Brook or to the point north of town.

The road at Old Brook Bridge became blocked at intervals; no cars could proceed in any direction at either location at the time that was set. The Tucker brother's bodies were cut down and they were lying side by side before the midnight hour in the morgue, by Chapman's Undertaking Establishment. The orders were made by Sheriff Maxwell.

Guy Martin went into the streets when the mob was dragging Michael. Guy described what he had witnessed with ultimate compassion to Alexander that next day, while they were sitting in his vehicle as he spoke. "There was this lady I knew and she had her three children with her to watch. She grabbed her youngest son, Bobby, and put his legs straddling her neck and told him to watch because you might have to do this one day."

My friends," Guy said down low. Then he spoke up, continuing, "I think the mob had taken his shirt off. A rope was around his neck and all the bones were gone from his face and chin. The bottom part of his face was flapping, and all the flesh was off his arms and his kneecaps were missing. His feet had turned over because he was dragged on his stomach. All of his skin and the top of his feet were off, along with some of his toes were gone." He stated, "I wish I never saw him as his eyes filled with tears." Guy was twenty-five years old at the time of this tragedy.

They all had been friends for a long time, now this was hard to swallow. Alexander replied, "You didn't have to say anything. That was a horrible way for anybody to leave this earth. It's hard listening to something like that flowing out of your mouth about friends of ours and it's true too."

Guy stated, "I talked with Mona earlier also."

Alexander knew the way that he was feeling was nothing

compared to what she must be going through.

"How was she holding up?"

Guy felt that she was doing what she had to do; she is a strong woman for sure. "I wanted her to hear it from one of us first." Guy stared out the window as he spoke saying, "Their bodies were laying on this object called a loose belt that's in the back room of the Mortuary. The loose belt started from the floor, running beside a long flight of stairs that goes up to the loft. When it's turned on it rotates, moving whatever is on it upward to the loft. That's where our friend's bodies were laid. Preceding an inquest was held. The Cardinals' jury consisted of six people, W. T. Holmes, Bruce Williams, J. R. Rudy, Michael Gilmore, H. M. Bernard, and T. B. Miller. They were the ones who pronounced Herbert Tucker dead from guns shot wounds inflicted by parties unknown and Michael Tucker death being dragged behind an Automobile that was driven by persons unknown. But I knew the driver was Billy Anderson."

Alexander couldn't believe what he had heard, "Did you say Billy Anderson?"

Guy reassured him; he did so hear him right. "Black, Billy Anderson, he works at the car lot, you know the motor company downtown. You know he didn't have a choice, but you know I couldn't have done it."

Alexander understood and he knew what he meant. "Their bodies were taken off to be buried, God knows where," As Guy Martin spoke and looked into Alexander's eyes his words were so sad, "Well I was just riding and I couldn't be still, now it's that time to go again. But you know we will meet later." Alexander repeated that he understood as they embraced, and Guy drove off.

With no respect or any decency for the two brothers, this creation was born.

A SILENT CRY FROM HEAVEN

A rampage of racial clusters surrounded us.
There was nowhere left to run and no reason to put up more of a fuss.

The lives we led before this day are now complete.
We thought we had promising futures, but we couldn't outrun this defeat.

The jealousy of those who felt we had too much,
robbed us of everything and left our families with not even a future to trust.
Even though we had no material items they wanted,
they always found reasons to kill us. So, we felt haunted.

Like a circus, they paraded us around town for all to see,
and hung our bodies lifelessly from a tree.

It was known that no Black man should be better off than any white man alive.
But we had to stand up for ourselves. We had to try.

Someone had to attempt to live a better life,
to overcome the ignorance and strife.
For our bodies were left uncovered.
Leaving us no dignity to muster.

Our families were never given the chance to say goodbye,
and no gravesite is present to visit or to sit beside.

Although no solid evidence of our stories
are apparent. Always know that we were there
and let their manipulative ways be transparent.

Continue to fight the lifelong struggle of racism,
because as long as there is a devil in hell, there
will always be someone there to challenge the truths we tell.

By: Crystal Quarles McDowell

The Lincoln County Times Stated:

The Presidents of the Ministerial Association call for Joint Action against Mob Violence, to be denounced. The Lincoln County Ministerial Association held its monthly gathering on Monday July 2nd. The editor released a formal statement that was handed to him by the Secretary. This was a process of resolving what had happened without any judgment, that was influenced by feeling in the words of the mass appeal.

Lynching is a crime no matter where it takes place and it make no different if you are a murderer or a thief. There is no reason why this should have taken place. The Federal should not come in between this event because there is no reason for them too. For more proof, this is a positive statement by the state's communities, and the counties of their incomparable force.

Here is the Resolution.

We the Brookhaven Ministerial Association do hereby go on record that the lawless mob action, which was displayed last Friday night in our community, the lynching of two Negroes.

We have expressed our sorrow and robustly denounce what was displayed last Friday night. We denounce the crime, but the two men were guilty. They should have been dealt with for the crime consequently to the crime provided by the law. We need to express our belief also.

When our officers and the law-abiding citizens had no interest or any measure taken to prevent harm during that day to stop this disgrace upon the name of our community when the mob lynching was threatened. We are extremely sorry for being in this situation.

We would like to make known that we are grateful for the results of the officers, the few that showed result and the citizens. Those individuals who pleaded to the mob not to carry out their purpose.

We hereby made known of our documented beliefs that the leaders of the mob together or with those who helped in breaking into the county jail and the lynching of the two Negros prisoners should be arrested and dealt with according to due procedures of the law, in order that the community and county know of the well understood terms to the country at large, our rejection of the mob actions.

We call upon all civic and religion organizations in the city and county for a formal statement expressing their opinion of sorrow or regret of the occurrence. We are inquiring a mass-meeting of law-abiding citizens of the town and country to be the town and country to be called on concerning the condemnation of the occurrence. In order for the whole country to know the attitude of our Christian citizenship and our young people may be led in a responsible manner, upholding the majesty?

Amos T. Richardson
President
C. G. May
Pressed in Regular Monthly
Session July 2, 1928

People of the Time

Alma Blunt, Haynes
Andy Howard
Anna Marie Case
Annie Bell Haynes, Quarles
Archie Alphonso Alexander
Aunt Helen
Billy Anderson
Brandon Case
Charlie O'Brian
Corey McDaniel
Curtis Haynes
Deputy Blunder
Eugene Smith
Frances Carter
Guy Martin
Hazel Haynes
Herbert Tucker
Howard Jackson
Jeremiah Pain
Judge G. E. Townsend
Lawrence Smith

Leo Haynes
Mandy Haynes
Marilyn Hardy
Marilee Pain
Mark Child
Mathew Hardy
Michael Tucker
Norman Harrison
Otis Smith
Ralph Haynes
Rev. Ned Owens
Rev. T. P. Newman
Robert E. Holmes
Sheriff Maxwell
Sheriff N. P. Taylor
Shug Caffie
Teddy E. Smith
Terry Hardy
Thomas Pain
Virgil Haynes

Reflections On Lynching

Remember:

There were mobs back in the days that hung Black men, and today there are still mobs. These mobs are now Black people and the only difference between the two are the Blacks are doing the same thing, but to each other. Have we turned this hate over to ourselves now?

www.ingramcontent.com/pod-product-compliance
Lightning Source LLC
Chambersburg PA
CBHW031017190726
48286CB00003BA/890

* 9 7 8 1 9 5 6 8 8 4 0 4 3 *